THE CONSPIRACY OF THE RAVENS

THE CONSPIRACY OF THE RAVENS

NELSON MCKEEBY

4 Horsemen Publications, Inc.
1497 Main St. Suite 169
Dunedin, FL 34698
4horsemenpublications.com
info@4horsemenpublications.com

Cover & Typesetting by Autumn Skye
Edited by Laura Mita

Library of Congress Control Number: 2023940183

Paperback ISBN-13: 979-8-8232-0233-6
Hardcover ISBN-13: 979-8-8232-0235-0
Audiobook ISBN-13: 979-8-8232-0232-9
Ebook ISBN-13: 979-8-8232-0234-3

TABLE OF CONTENTS

THE BOY WHO ATE THOMAS CUSTER'S HEART

DATE: JULY 26, 1876
LOCATION: FRESH WELLS, INDIAN TERRITORY

Blue Flower gazed down at the youth. He was maybe fifteen, dirty, malnourished with whipcord muscles, and a fading bruise on his face. The boy was a vision of the grasslands washed up on Blue Flower's doorstep as if a stick carried on a rain-swelled stream, damaged by the currents that had forced him forward and back, but not yet destroyed, and stamped with the defiance of his people. On the dusty horizon, the Quakers who had left him were rapidly disappearing into the stormy, red sunset.

"Marlow!" She yelled for her husband.

Marlow Smith had shed his tribal name and worked as a bookkeeper for the agency. His coworkers said if only the naphtha soap would wash his skin just a little better, he would be as good as white. He dealt with the insult because they were not starving, nor were the blue soldiers gunning them down as they were to the North in revenge for the murder of the Morning Star. Some of her neighbors mourned this blond warrior, but not Blue Flower. She remembered the government soldiers in a way her husband never could with his education and letters. She remembered the knives they carried on the ends of their muskets, the blankness in their eyes as they killed women and children for doing nothing more than existing. Marlow could never comprehend the hell she wished to send the white soldiers to.

Marlow came out and paused as he took in the sight of the boy and the rapidly retreating Quakers. He was dressed in a casual work suit consisting of an engineer's coat, pleated trousers, a white shirt with a stiff collar attached, and a pair of small glasses pushed up on his head. "Did they not want to have tea?"

"No, they just dropped off this." Her nod at the boy was curt at best.

Marlow focused on the man-child, a creature with a hunted, foxlike demeanor and a visage sketched on his face that could kill worlds. Despite the hate in his eyes, the child started crying under the intense gaze of the couple. It was also obvious he was not Cherokee.

"He is not of the band!" Marlow exclaimed. Whites claimed that Indians looked alike, but it was not true. Tribes differed in how they carried themselves. A Lakota had a wide gait and swung his arms farther out when he walked. A Cherokee was more parsimonious in his movements and gestures. A Hopi would sometimes conceal their hands and arms under their clothing, while eastern bands never put their hands in their pockets unless they lived close by a white community. Blue Flower could see her husband assess the child. This was a youth of the grasslands whose mind was a mobile canvas that would refuse any paint that could narrow down his world. Marlow must be thinking that there was very little labor to be had from a child of the grasslands. He would eat their food, run wild in the town, and bring ruin on them unless they could tame his wild impulses and help him survive in the white world. Marlow continued to talk after a long lapse. “Why would they bring a Lakota to us?”

Blue Flower replied, “We look the same to the whites, do we not?”

Marlow frowned at her. He had business with the Quakers, relied on them to ease business with the blue coats. He was unhappy she did not like them. She knew enough of his feelings now that even a slight change in his tone communicated what others might need days to understand. Blue Flower was not a lover of the spoken word. She lived in a world of modulated silences where the creak of a board meant her husband was uneasy over some question of profits, where the sound of the watermill slowing up could indicate that the water tank would not fill that night, and the laughter of children would indicate her own mind wandering to the three shrines that sat behind the house, each one a memory of a bright smile and a warm hug.

“Do you speak the language?” Marlow asked in Cherokee. The youth continued to cry, showing no signs of understanding. “English?” he asked, and the child nodded.

“We will call you a-tlo-yi-hv a-yo-li; it means cry-baby. At least until you learn to speak up for yourself.”

The youth nodded, tears dripping dirty water down his face. Blue Flower would think the Quakers might have bathed him or dressed him in better clothing before throwing the foundling onto their stoop. Marlow thought the Quakers were saints because they would loan Indians money at just twice what they loaned whites.

She stepped in front of her husband's dilatory questioning. "So, did they let you keep anything?" She hoped he would have some money to purchase respectable clothing. Missionaries were strange that way. They would watch silently as soldiers robbed you blind, killed your children, and burned your homes, but would then gather money and food for the person they had just seen ruined.

From deep in the folds of his ragged garments, the youth pulled a large, shiny silver revolver of the newest make. Blue Flower grabbed her husband and drew him back as he let out a convulsive oath. "Give that damn thing to me!" he yelled.

The youth seemed to grow two feet in stature even as tears continued to fall from his eyes. "I took this from the brother of the Morning Star after counting coup on him in battle. I will die before I will let you or anyone else take it from me."

Blue Flower stepped in front of her husband. "Fool boy, keep the gun, but never show it to anyone. They are killing Indians who even talk like that."

The youth seemed to deflate. "I am a man! I counted coup in battle."

Blue Flower reached out and slapped the youth. "And now you are a child again. Learn to keep your mouth shut and your eyes open, and you may live to the next winter. Otherwise, I will have to bury you with the rest of my sons, and the sky knows I do not want another grave."

The youth hid the gun back in his rags and said nothing else. Behind him, Blue Flower noted a storm brewing up and hoped it was not an omen about the child's life.

INCIDENT AT BASHFUL

DATE: AUGUST 7, 1960
LOCATION: BASHFUL, KANSAS

The purple 1957 Chevy blasted across the sunbaked Kansas landscape, sometimes hitting 120 km/h on straights. Despite the reputation she had earned for reluctant obedience in the motor pool, today she was on her best behavior, hugging the road like a race car and paying close attention to each rise and fall of the pavement. Her engine purred with the low-throttled roar of restrained power, wheel ready and responsive like the stick of the most modern Delta Dart fighter.

Ivy was in a mood. Maybe it was the stupid mission of picking up some girl in a tiny Kansas town and driving her to an even tinier Wyoming town. Maybe it was the haunting dreams of Indochina that twisted his brain most nights. He could almost taste the smell of rotting plants and hear the blistering, mind-numbing heat that cracked the skin and drove men away from their intellects. That terrible land had finally broken his mind and left him ... nothing, except to contemplate the car he was driving and the town he was driving to.

"The Company" had gone all out on the balky Chevy. It had power steering, power brakes, a V8 with fuel injectors, three-point harness belts, safety glass, an air conditioner, and a heater with three extra coils for Arctic weather. The radio was not only equipped with a powerful A.M. receiver but also had a crystal to listen in on local police chatter between radio-equipped patrol cars and their dispatchers. In Bashful, the dispatcher was a soft contralto named Betty-Jean Weyerhaeuser who called the town's three officers, Bud, Ted, and Charlie, by their first names. To make the driving experience more relaxing, it had a Turboglide automatic transmission, and installed on the passenger-side dash was a highly disturbing electric clock.

Perhaps the most amazing thing attached to the Chevy was that damned clock. As far as Ivy could tell, it dropped less than a second a day. He had given up setting it to his Rolex Oyster Perpetual (with a face that read 50 m = 165 feet so science-ignorant Americans could time athletic events) and started to set the Rolex to the car. The clock brought a preternatural precision to the Chevy that should not exist in a hunk of metal. Approximate left the realm of reality and retreated into the darkness of the night given the accuracy of the clock. With the Chevy, time was so accurate that the universe had to set its clocks to it.

Contemplating the radio made Ivy think also of the car's unusual trunk. In the capacious trunk of the Chevy, "the Company" had provided two portable "Snap On" transit cases for the things agents carried to help them stay alive. "Leave the car and take the cases" was the rule when things got tight.

The cases were large and looked as if they might not fit in the trunk, but when they were inside, there was still room for Ivy and Rains-a-Lot to throw in their own steamer trunks, a couple of duffle bags, a spare tire, a rain tarp and a canvas tent, a box of spare parts, a tool kit, and several cases of army rations. When they had first been given the car last year, they had stacked all their desired dunnage next to it. The stack had towered above the car, but somehow it had all fit in the truck with room for a little more.

The trunk and the clock were not all that was wrongfully right about the vehicle "the Company" had given them. In some ways, there was no give in the purple Chevy. When dirt had covered its sides or its tires grew caked in mud, she would be hard to start, would hesitate in acceleration, get squishy in braking, would idle like a pig, and would complain about the smallest use of power with a flurry of pings and sighs. Ivy had thus learned to keep the purple Chevy spotless. He would wash the car with a shammy and soft soap, buff the windows until they were invisible, carefully degrease and buff the engine compartment and replace any hoses that looked even a little suspect.

The Chevy had fuel injection, like fighter jets have, so most mechanics would not touch her. Instead, Ivy had taken to a constant round of inspections and cleanings of the entire engine. Deep in some corner of his mind, he felt a purple satisfaction from his efforts, and that made him even happier when the Chevy sparkled. After a few hours washing the car, buffing the seats, shampooing the carpets, and giving the engine some care, she would drive like a dream. Causality was challenged in the charging metal beast.

When the car drove well like today, it was a good thing, because the Midwest was an endless canvas of sameness repeated to a horizon that came too quickly and dwarfed any structure that man in his hubris tried to make. "Big-sky-country" they called it. Ivy thought it was more like "long-road-country" with miles and miles for miles and miles and nothing else to ease the severity of the landscape or to soften the imagination. Kansas alone, one damn state in the endless middle of America, was one-third of France in area. And almost no one lived here.

Tornadoes had passed through this area just a month ago, leaving their signs in unexpected places. Unseasonable damn things that wandered across the landscape as if controlled by some maniacal intellect. It was the barns that scarred Ivy in his soul. Every couple of kilometers there was a destroyed barn with its roof sitting intact adjacent. Nature, in its terrible majesty, had somehow directed the tornadoes with a horrible precision that preserved the roof of a structure but destroyed everything the roof concealed. It was like a bad joke. Some farmer coming out of his basement would see the death of all he owned, but at least he had all the slate shingles he needed in case he wanted to rebuild.

Rains-a-Lot sat next to Ivy in quiet, stern confidence. Ivy's partner did not appreciate all the details of technology or worry about oddities of weather. He treated the Chevy, with all its quirks, like a fine horse. He had never known the stern man to use a telephone, send a telegraph, or turn on a television set. Gizmos did not seem to matter to him much. Ivy doubted Rains-a-Lot processed the differences between the new Chevy and the old Packard they had been assigned in any qualitative sense. To him, the car was like a steed that, sadly, he had never learned to control but could still ride in.

The car took air over a frost heave, and for a second, there was that feeling of emptiness as they traced an ogive through space, until they landed with a thud and the rear tires caught the pavement with a rubbery growl. Rains-a-Lot continued to look forward, but his ears moved a little, a sign of tension. Although Rains-a-Lot did not drive, he did not approve of Ivy's driving much of the time either. Ivy knew he let silly things bother him, and through some Gallic genetic trait, those irritations were transmitted to his feet and legs through muscle memory. When Ivy drove calmly, the Indian would roll down his window and put his head on a swivel, looking at each extraneous detail that passed them, as if the red-painted mailboxes or square bale hay could suddenly pose an existential threat to a car rocketing down the street. When Ivy was disturbed, he drove faster and more erratically, causing Rains-a-Lot to fix his head forward and grasp at the base of his seat, as if he were worried the forces of acceleration might tear him apart. This in turn made Ivy more upset with the world, and he would actually find himself driving worse to see if the Indian would react.

The Kansas day was hot, "La-Rue-Sans-Joie" hot, although without the sickeningly sweet smell of decay or the humidity that would kill a man who was unprepared to tend the basic mechanics of living. Ivy blasted the Chevy over a bridge, nearly taking it airborne again, using the car as some turgid expression of his mental ill-ease. Rains-a-Lot made a huffing sound as the vehicle skidded slightly on its big, black, all-weather tires and turned his gaze to Ivy. He could feel his partner's stare saying, "That was too much even for you." It was a rebuke of unprofessional behavior that Rains-a-Lot would provide him only on the rarest occasion. Ivy glanced at his passenger and purposely crinkled his eyebrows in reply to the Indian's stare. Rains-a-Lot called Ivy's emotional driving "méthode française," as if it was something Ivy could change. Of course, knowing the Cherokee's exact feelings on any subject was an issue of delicacy. Calling the Indian taciturn did not begin to explain his ability to avoid the use of any language for weeks at a time. Still, after two years Ivy had learned that Rains-a-Lot talked with a language of stillness that was rich in its ability to communicate to those who listened. Right now, his face tightened at the cheeks, which might have been meant to say, "Just do your job and leave the bullshit back in the hotel room with the bottles of gin."

Rains-a-Lot was not that angry with Ivy, but he was concerned. What made him concerned was the mission, and Ivy's mood, the dry, hot air of the dusty plains, and that feeling like there were words to be said, although none ever came. It was the feedback loop that Ivy felt them in, Rains-a-Lot's anxiety fed Ivy's disquiet, which fed back into the Indian's mood and sent the Chevy speeding nearly 120 km/h down the road to a tiny town. *Shake it off and think on something else,* Ivy thought. But it was possible for him to not imagine they were the villains in some cheap and sordid spy novel written by a college student in need of something to turn in for their English class. Ivy had done too much in his life to ever think of himself as a white hat. Besides, he had a scar on his face and would never lose the edges of his French accent, so he often felt tailor-made for the role of villain.

He went into a reverie.

Ivy had met the *James Bond* author Ian Fleming in the war before he was anything more than a reckless teenage minder for the French resistance. The older man was somewhat of a pig to the younger Ivy.

As a youth, Ivy was proud and traumatized from four years of fighting. The death of so many people he cared for had marked him. He had become easily hurt by uncaring adults. Fleming was just the sort of uncaring nonce that a child-like Ivy could teethe at, all British and self-centered in the maelstrom of war.

Years later, he had read Fleming's novel *Dr. No* while recovering from battle injuries in Saigon, and he thought of how much of a scam the spook's books were. Anyone who read the thing would not actually know Bond was Fleming, just some fantasy version of him wrapped in a thrilling alter ego.

Ivy knew the real Fleming though. He remembered the man's goddamned bouncy jeep speeding across the countryside risking his life and those with him. Ivy, as a member of the resistance, would have preferred to remain unseen, to blend in with the world, to avoid eyes that might tell tales to fascist killers. Fleming though was to Ivy the textbook definition of a goddamned amateur.

Despite the contempt he felt for the man, some of his ways had rubbed off on Ivy. He had learned to drink the gin Fleming had pushed onto him, and Fleming's fatalistic way of seeing the world in black and white had become part of Ivy's worldview. Ivy never thought of it as a good exchange of values and wondered if everyone learned the wrong things from their patrons.

A turn in the road came up, suddenly jerking Ivy from his thoughts; he had to overcorrect to avoid bouncing into a ditch. Sometimes he lived more in the past than the now, his brain a broken instrument that was always split in time. There was mental scar tissue that seemed to prevent him from ever being a whole person.

Ivy glanced again at his partner. He was older than Ivy by about ten years, a nearly silent stoic who was scrutable and known to him, if to few other people. He wore his heart on his sleeve, exposed to the cruelties of the world, but he was a person of such strength that he had long ago found ways of hiding this "weakness." It was not a weakness at all in Ivy's mind that Rains-a-Lot cared deeply. His chagrin at Ivy's emotional state was just that, caring. As the Kansas landscape whipped past, Ivy thought that he never would have survived joining "the Company" if not for Rains-a-Lot and his silent love.

The hot summer wind whipped into the car through the open windows. Ivy's erratic driving had caused Rains-a-Lot to move his hands from clutching the seat to having one hand on his hat and the other on the door jam. Ivy came up behind a tractor and sloughed around it with squealing tires and a sense that the vehicle could topple over under the force of the maneuver. Again Ivy felt Rains-a-Lot's stare. When he glanced back at the Indian, he saw the man's eyes were squinted in a narrow squint as if to say, "Find a way to keep it together today."

Ivy nodded, acknowledging he was troubled, and slowed down. A deep purple thought in the back of his head seemed to thank him on behalf of the Chevy as if a car could give psychic voice to thanks. Next to Ivy, he could feel Rains-a-Lot remove his death grip on the door and take the opportunity to remove the hat from his head. Out of the corner of his eye, Ivy saw the Indian carefully work out a few blemishes in the hat's cloth.

He was an athletic man, looking much like Jay Silverheels with thick, black hair, beautiful sun-touched skin, and an angular, muscular face, but he had no vanity for his physical appearance. His only real self-conceit was the hat. Unlike skin, muscles, and bone, which could not be changed, Rains-a-Lot obviously was proud of how the hat made him look and feel, and hats could and should be changed from time to time, at least in the Indian's mind.

"Your hat is new," Ivy said. It was a gambit. A distraction from memory, from the oppressive big sky, from demolished barns simmering in the summer heat, and from a road that threw too many sudden curves at a driver.

Rains-a-Lot regarded his new Stetson fedora, manipulating it again in his hands. "Bing Crosby," he replied. The hat was brown with a tan silk accent into which a single wisp of a feather had been placed. It was dimpled left, right, and on top, and it had been brushed with a light saddle brush until it gleamed. Ivy knew he had blocked the hat to keep it in perfect shape as often as he could, usually when he was hand-loading ammunition in hotel rooms. When Rains-a-Lot acquired a new hat it became his single point of pride, and he took as good care of them as he did of his antique silver revolver.

Dustin-Rhodes Corporation was big on conformity and performing a mission with precision, which is one thing that made Rains-a-Lot an odd partner.

The manual for Troubleshooters clearly stated that each member of this branch was a public representative of "the Company" that should dress always according to standards, which the Indian never did. Instead, he wore his brown Stetson (or whatever fashionable hat he had chosen that month), a brown leather flyer's jacket, a white cotton shirt with red and blue stripes, and green pleated pants covering subdued cavalry boots. He did not even own a charcoal suit or pretend uniformity mattered. He was so good though that Central never bitched about the dress code with him. Rains-a-Lot was considered an old-timer in the Troubleshooter pool and had a certain flare that gave him a pass on such things.

Rains-a-Lot's outfit was far more sensible than "the Company"-mandated charcoal, double-breasted ring jackets with exaggerated Madison Avenue shoulders and the pleated, ankle-hugging slacks that made Ivy look like an absurd triangle. The shoes were the biggest pain in the ass—leather-soled black brogues, which were impossible to run in unless you took a belt sander to their heels and toes. The grey pork pie hats that were the standard issue could have been nice, but they were a bit too small for Ivy's head and were immediately lost in any chase. That was nine dollars out of his paycheck every time he had to purchase a replacement. It was almost like "the Company" wanted Troubleshooters to stick out. He had always figured it was like a tiger being orange. Just throw on some stripes and tigers own any plot of land they live in. No one else gets to be orange.

Of course, if the tiger had to wear leather-soled brogues, he would spend all his time tripping on his face and starving while the little forest deer laughed their asses off in the safety of the next clearing.

Ivy nodded again at the Indian's hat. "Bet you look like Bing Crosby wearing it."

Rains-a-Lot chuffed. It was his version of laughter.

Satisfied he had done his job to make conversation, Ivy turned away. Rains-a-Lot's pride about the hat was just another dimension of the man's character that a stranger would never fathom. Ivy loved the movies and dragged his partner to them as often as he could. The Indian mostly ignored the storylines, but he would marvel at the hats he saw in them. If an actor in a movie showed up sporting a new style of hat, Rains-a-Lot would notice. Soon, he would own one of the same hats. It was one of the reasons Ivy had skipped *Ben Hur*—from fear that Rains-a-Lot would channel Hugh Griffith and wind up with a keffiyeh as his next hat.

Bashful came up suddenly, the speed limit dropping to 25 mph, causing the Chevy to let out a purple groan as Ivy tested its massive brakes. The presence of a police officer in a clunky Ford radio car showed the inconvenient placement of the sign was a strategy. Despite slowing with every impressive ounce of braking power the Chevy had, it still tore past the police car at 80 km/h. Ivy's speed was rewarded with flashing lights and a whining siren. He heard a small snick next to him. His partner was brass checking his Smith and Wesson Model 3 and placing it on his lap under his hat.

Ivy tugged the wheel of the car and abruptly pulled it to the side, then slammed the transmission into park as soon as the car skidded to a stop. He rubbed his face with the palms of his hands, removing a layer of sweat and dust that had been building up for 70 kilometers. Once the cool wind of the road was gone, the air streaming in the window became sticky and superheated. The smell of gasoline, road tar, cow shit, and some sort of greasy cooking assaulted his sense of smell, while dust that had been trailing the car for hundreds of kilometers caught up to them in a roiling cloud. He reached down and turned off the scanner as the officer walked up.

The cop was a younger man, but he already had the second stripe of a senior officer. By some cosmic coincidence, the name on his plate said, "Weyerhaeuser, C." Ivy placed both of his hands on the steering wheel and said, "Officer Weyerhaeuser, may I help you?"

"Fancy car. You know how fast you were going?"

Ivy nodded. "Yes, Officer Weyerhaeuser, this car has a speedometer."

"Well, you were going over the speed limit. I need your license and paperwork. And make sure Tonto shows me his BIA registration. He will need to tell us whether he spends the night, we have rules about Indians in town past dark."

Ivy felt a growl building in his brain, that growl that said his self-control was limited. *Go ahead son*, he thought, *flick that scar tissue some.* Even as the thought crossed his mind, a purple thought tamped it down. Instead of pulling the man-child down by his tie and beating his face against the door, Ivy said, "I am reaching in my jacket for my credentials."

"Sure thing, bub." The officer was way out of position for a traffic stop. His knees were vulnerable to a door smash, he was bending over trying to get a look at Rains-a-Lot, leaving his tie only inches from Ivy's left hand, and his pistol, riding low on his right hip, was nicely positioned if Ivy decided to snatch it out and use it against its owner. He was screaming "amateur" on so many levels that Ivy almost decided that Darwinism must be a myth. If it was not, then someone this dumb would have been eaten by dogs before he was three.

Ivy's own Browning hung upside down in a wire spring and canvas shoulder holster, made by an old man at the Boyt Harness Company just for him. As he reached his hand under his jacket, his fingers brushed the automatic and the small knife that hung next to it. There was a second of existential danger for the officer that he would never know he went through. Instead of the pistol though, Ivy's fingers pulled the black leather credentials wallet he carried in his jacket pocket and presented it to "Weyerhaeuser, C" in a single, fluid motion.

"John Jones, Jr., Federal Bureau of Investigation," he said, two lies for the price of one today.

The officer's voice rose an octave. "No kidding, I would never have figured that with your accent. Where are you from?"

"New Jersey. You can never outgrow that accent." Ivy paused for a second and thought, *Idiot.*

The officer swiveled his head around as if he were suddenly in a spy movie. "Yeah, I hear yah. What are you doing around here?"

Ivy replied, "I am picking up a witness. You understand that I cannot reveal operational details."

"No, no, never." The officer's voice got really low. "What about the Indian though." He seemed to be under the impression that Ivy's passenger could not hear what was being said. Of course, the child had not bothered to note the passenger had a hat in his lap. Ivy imagined the revolver filled with shells, hand-loaded with black powder, the lead bullets for each round inserted backward with the base hollowed out. Despite all that power in his hand, Rains-a-Lot would never act unprofessionally. Not to the extent of airing out some poor idiot for being racist and dumb. In fact, he could imagine his partner risking his life to save the little prick. That did not reduce the irony that the kid was breathing from moment to moment only by the forbearance of an Indian.

Ivy looked intently at the officer and said, "What Indian?"

"The one sitting next to you." The kid's voice sounded frustrated, as if he could not call Ivy's attention to a baby elephant.

Ivy turned and made a small finger gesture, drawing the officer in close. Matching his quiet tone of voice, he said, "Shhh, he is clandestine. You want to blow his cover?"

"Geez, sir, sorry, he's not really an Indian?"

"He is as American as I am," Ivy replied ironically.

"Why is he not talking?" The officer asked.

Ivy turned his gaze to Rains-a-Lot. His partner had a slight tightening of his lower jaw, which he used for a smile. "My partner's accent is a giveaway." The tightening grew more pronounced, and a crease dimpled between his eyes. That was Rains-a-Lot laughing hysterically.

The young officer rubbed his face as if he had a beard. "He from Jersey, also?"

"As far as you know," Ivy replied. Rains-a-Lot chuffed, then turned it into a slight cough.

"I have to tell my father about this." The officer seemed to be mystified but satisfied.

Ivy replied, "Only official contacts, I am sorry."

"My father is the police chief," the officer said.

Ivy nodded fatalistically, "Of course he is. We will be picking up the daughter of a witness and leaving your jurisdiction. Should be a cakewalk." He looked at the sky and said, "Good weather at least."

The officer adjusted his gun belt and stood up straight. "Should be perfect weather, sir. Nice to have met you, Agent Jones."

Ivy waved at the officer as he walked back to his radio car. Then he flipped on the Chevy's police-scanner and heard the officer report to his sister, Ms. Betty Jean Weyerhaeuser, about the arrival of strangers, asking her to tell their father Big Jed that he had something very exciting to tell him. Next to him, Rains-a-Lot listened and watched with stern, staring eyes. When the patrol car had carried the young officer away, he took his hat from his lap, revealing the revolver that had been sitting there. He then screwed the hat onto his head about a centimeter past where fashion dictated.

Ivy regarded the weapon in the Indian's lap. It was an ancient Smith and Wesson Model 3 that fired black powder cartridges. Rains-a-Lot cared for the pistol as if it were a family heirloom, constantly fitting, refitting, and replacing parts on the pistol. He even handmade his own ammunition, spending a few evenings a month pulling apart commercial .45 Colt rounds, filing and clipping the cases to shorten them for the revolver's smaller cylinder, re-swaging the lead bullets, tossing away the smokeless gunpowder and replacing it with black powder he made in hotel sinks. If death was an art form, Rains-a-Lot was a master of its expression.

The Indian must have felt Ivy staring at him. He stared back as if to say, "Nothing wrong with being cautious." Ivy let his eyebrows raise a little, implying that shooting the cop would be a bit over the top. The Indian shook his head and turned away, pocketing his revolver, implying it was more likely Ivy would have done violence to the idiot kid than Rains-a-Lot. Ivy never won wordless arguments with his partner.

Bashful was a whistle-stop if you did not blow the whistle too long. The town was a cluster of buildings huddled together around a town square, trailing off into four-dozen private homes. At no point were you out of sight of the corn fields that were probably the most important business of the town. At the edge of the town center, they passed two large silos sitting by a railroad siding and then a pair of big canneries, each of which must have employed fifty or more locals. So what was Kelle Brainerd, target of "the Company," doing in this place?

He had read her file that morning. Ms. Brainerd had sent a letter to the FBI making certain assertions and claims that had immediately seen the correspondence transferred to file thirteen. File thirteen was a reference for the garbage can, normal bureaucratic talk. At the Bureau, the file was outsourced to Dustin-Rhodes, the official name for what its employees simply called "the Company," never omitting a capital C or the quotation marks. Somewhere in the endless maze of bureaucracy (which rumor said mostly consisted of accountants and mathematicians in tiny rooms all linked by sixteen huge computers) a faceless drone had connected

Ms. Brainerd's letter with some other bits of data and decided to invite her in for an all-expenses-paid trip to the metropolis of Hulett, Wyoming (population 333), on the steep banks of the Belle Fourche River for a debrief. The information she had must have been important, or there was an element of danger to her or "the Company;" otherwise, Troubleshooters would not have been the ones called on to collect her.

The young Ms. Brainerd was not expected to object to her vacation, or else Central would have called it a snatch. Central was short for Central Dispatch, the main organization within Dustin-Rhodes Company that connected corporate resources with problems; its purpose was having one solve the other. If your toilets clogged at your small animal study lab in Newberry, South Carolina, Central would arrange for their repair. In some ways, Troubleshooters were just toilet repair people, and if faced with a clogged toilet, they would cheerfully clean the device and return it to working order. Troubleshooters though were at the very top of corporate hierarchy. If plumbers were the equivalent of a hammer, then Troubleshooters were phased plasma rifles in the 40-watt range.

The town center was based on a square and a few blocks of business fronts and stately homes. Like many small towns, Bashful was "zoned" after a fashion, but the zones were so small that they could consist of only a few lots before giving way to the next zone. The business district was the square and two of the streets that radiated outward; it also included the police station, a small medical center, the town office building, a state and federal service building, and the military recruiter's office. A small number of downtown hotels, hostels, or apartment buildings backed onto the business district, each a tiny structure connected to its neighbor by a common wall. Then came a layer of private houses that stood free from each other but used most of their plots. Unlike the more rural spaces around Bashful, the houses and buildings in town were packed together as if to protect themselves from an existential evil that lurked in the farmlands.

The density of housing and the requirements of parking caused the speed limits to fall with cars coming and going from spots stopping the flow of traffic altogether. The Chevy was unhappy moving through town—its engine designed more to roar across the countryside than idle through streets. Despite this, it was tuned almost silent in low idle, a mechanical panther prowling herds of Midwestern wildebeests.

The town square, a grassy plot at the epicenter of the community, was busy, filled with running children and the elderly who were either lawn bowling or playing shoddy games of chess on cement tables with the chess boards permanently etched in the stone. Ivy pulled the car in by a brass twelve-pounder Napoleon, being cared for by an "at-large" inmate dressed in prison garb. Probably a hobo who was arrested as an excuse to give him odd jobs and feed him a few meals. And in the middle of the park, sitting on a tartan blanket, was their target. It was the first time Ivy had seen Kelle Brainerd in person.

She was petite, maybe 150 centimeters tall, and probably not even 50 kilograms in mass. She had dark, black hair, cut boyish short and held in place by metal hair clips. She was wearing a pink poodle skirt with a black appliqué poodle prominent on the front, black and white saddle shoes in shiny patent leather, and a grey sweatshirt that said, "College" on it. It was odd that it did not say what college was being referred to, that the word was enough for the person who had made it.

The girl appeared to be fifteen but was reading a huge university-level textbook of some sort, labeled as a library checkout. Beside her was an Aladdin Industries vacuum flask and lunchbox with the image of Hopalong Cassidy fixed to the metal. She also had a huge blue backpack with a brushed metal frame she leaned against, an impossibly large thing for a girl her size, made of some space-age blue fabric. It looked like a square satellite dish.

Rains-a-Lot stepped from the car and went off around the park. He was the spotter while Ivy made contact. The park itself had too many moving pieces to keep track of them all, although Ivy tried. He imagined for a second that the old chess players were concealing Bren guns, or that the children had been equipped with bombs, but he quickly shook it off. He needed a drink, but it would be several days before he could have one. His bottles of Bénédictine and Gordon's Gin were waiting for him in his personal chest in the Chevy, but he could not open it because Rains-a-Lot had the key.

Ivy walked up to the girl as she read. She looked like someone's rebellious daughter rather than a target of interest for "the Company." At thirty-two, Ivy was already seeing himself as ancient, a person who had seen too much. But that also made him see children as people he should protect. He was not sure how he would have reacted if this was a snatch. There was always that internal turmoil of what to do if "the Company" ordered you to take a bridge too far.

The girl glanced up at him and said, "What are you supposed to be, Men in Charcoal?"

Ivy goggled for a second. What did she say? The girl was already throwing stuff into her pack: thermos, lunch box, and book. "Sorry, wrong snappy reference." She switched to an awful James Cagney voice, "Look here G-Man, badge me and get it over with, see?"

The ground cloth went into the backpack last. Ivy saw it was packed with canvas sacks filled tightly with smaller objects, like notebooks packaged in elastic and bundles of clothing. A slick compression sack held a bulging Arctic sleeping bag, while a puffy coat was slung on the top. She lifted the huge pack up as if she were a weightlifter and then stared at him.

Ivy had been taught by Rains-a-Lot to enjoy movies and was fascinated at how actors in the movies could snap off dialogue, knowing what to say at just the right time, but his own attempts always fell a little flat. "Did you know we would be picking you up?" was the best he could muster.

"Nope, I always read in the park with an expedition pack." Some of the old men had stopped their chess game and were listening. A couple was pushing a stroller by the cannon and had stopped to chat with the trustee. In the far distance, music from an ice cream truck rang out across Bashful. A siren sounded as Officer Weyerhaeuser made a new stop at his traffic blind, while in a nearby shop, a record player drilled out "Chantilly Lace" with a lenticular wobble indicating a warped recording.

Rains-a-Lot walked up. He made a sign by tapping his inside wrist. It meant "someone is watching." The girl started humming the song playing in the distance as she fidgeted with her pack.

Ivy covertly snuck a glance. There was a man in a watch cap staring at them. Ivy glanced back at Rains-a-Lot and put his finger on his cheek, causing his partner to stiffen slightly. It was their sign of possible trouble in public.

"If you guys are going Brokeback on me, wait until I charge my iPhone, I want to shoot video of it. Ten thousand hits on YouTube at least." The girl said. It was gibberish that hurt his head to hear.

Ivy tried to break into the stream of nonsense but failed. It was like Ms. Brainerd was speaking a foreign language. There was no context to it. "You sent a letter. Will you come with us?" he finally said.

"Actually I was planning to visit Storm Lake and put flowers on the Big Bopper's grave, but since you both showed up and asked so nicely, I would love to come with you," she replied.

Ivy looked back at the man in the watch cap. He nodded to Rains-a-Lot, who looked at the sky while a frown sketched his face. "Ms. Brainerd, there is some urgency. Can you go to the purple Chevy parked by the cannon?"

She looked at Ivy as though he were an idiot. "Of course."

Across the park, heat waves from the blazing summer caused the sky to shimmer. The man in the knit cap began to walk forward through a group of children playing under the watchful eyes of their caretakers. He was dressed head-to-toe in soft leather buckskins and had a broom in his hand. The girl noticed Ivy staring past her and turned around as gracefully as a hippo. "Crap, you lead him here!"

Rains-a-Lot reached into his jacket for his pistol. The wind was picking up in the park, blowing leaves around and causing a few of the people to retreat into the surrounding stores, fearing a sudden summer storm.

The man walked straight to them. Ivy stepped forward and said, "You should stop."

"The girl is my property." The man said. His voice had a timbre with a strange reverb to it, as though it was made up of hundreds of violin strings being plucked. Little crackles of electricity were flowing around him.

One of the old men at the table must have heard that. He stood up, cane in hand, and hobbled over. "Did you just say that cute little girl belonged to you?"

"Yeah, fuck that," Kelle said. She balled her fists and turned around. Ivy stepped back a few steps and stopped her with his left hand, reaching under his suit coat with his right.

The man in the cap, distracted for a second, said, "Shut up, old man."

The old man was wearing a little sash of medals and a white hat that said, "4th Iowa Militia, Prairie City, NCOIC." He was obviously some retired soldier, although his medals and the significance of the unit he was claiming missed Ivy. He did not like being spoken to that way, as evidenced by a dark cloud crossing his face.

The man in the watch cap continued to walk forward toward them. In his wake, the winds increased as if they were in some way being commanded to rise. The people who, a second ago, had been playing in the sun began to retreat as their blankets and picnic supplies were lashed by the wind, leaving the strange man in the knit cap in control of much of the grass-covered town center. As he approached, the old veteran clenched his fists on a stick, seething at being insulted. The man in the cap stopped in front of him, a mocking laugh on his lips, which caused the old veteran to take his ersatz weapon, nothing more than a walking cane, and smack the impudent stranger on the head. The man's cap fell off and revealed pointed ears, a bald and heavily tattooed skull, and two immense and painful-looking earrings. Revealed to the world, the strange man screamed and brought up his staff. Lighting began to flicker around his body and a wind started to whip around them as if he were calling a tornado.

The old veteran said, "Martians! Fuck this!" and turned tail to run off. Ivy stepped forward to cover the man's retreat and give Rains-a-Lot time to get the girl away.

"I will suck your soul, weak one!" the creature yelled, turning to Ivy. He was humanoid in most dimensions, but the illusion that he was human was no longer supportable. He seemed to be Darkness and grow in the flashes of light, while a low rumble could be heard, perhaps a preternatural thunder. Rains-a-Lot stepped up and fired five rapid shots from his Schofield, knocking the malevolent man back.

The girl screamed, "That won't do any good."

"Fuck this" was right, Ivy thought. He grabbed Kelle and manhandled her back to the car, throwing her and her pack into the back. When she tried to get out, he looked at her as sternly as he could. She stared back, angry but also a bit scared. Ivy knew exactly what she

was thinking because he was thinking the same. *Fight the guy who scares you. Do not back down.*

He slammed the back door and jumped into the driver's seat. The Chevy roared to life in the darkened eave of the storm, Ivy so nervous it took him a second to note that he had failed to put the key in the ignition. *Damn weird car that would start without a key,* Ivy thought.

The dark man was standing again as if the five bullets fired into his chest were not a big deal, facing down Rains-a-Lot who had returned his pistol to its holster and had drawn a huge Bowie knife, glinting blue in the swirling storm-occluded light.

Ivy slammed on the gas and the Chevy bounced over the curb into the park, causing the poor cannon-polishing trustee to leap over his black-painted brass charge and duck for safety. All around the park, old men hiding underneath chess tables abandoned them and fled behind trees. The Chevy's big tires bit into the park's green grass, slewing the car's rear axle in a series of fishtails. Ivy used the last fishtail to sweep the strange creature off his feet while giving Rains-a-Lot a chance to dive into the open passenger's window. The creature leapt twenty meters into the air, broom outstretched and hand wrapped around a bolt of cracking energy, but Rains-a-Lot was able to make it into the car in a single Olympic-quality dive. Hearing his partner buckle in, Ivy gave the Chevy gas, laying a line of rubber out of the square and down the main street.

"Who is that guy?" Ivy yelled.

The girl said, "David Lo Pan? How the hell should I know his name?" Ivy sensed she was lying, but this was not the time to figure things out. Ivy affixed the name David Lo Pan to the flying man with the broom as better than any he could assign and looked back over his shoulder.

The threatening storm roiled in the sky as they tore away from the town proper and down a backroad. Ivy spun from one side street to another, gaining psychological distance without quitting the town. His goal was to give them a short respite to gather their wits instead of fleeing haphazardly from civilization.

"The Company" abhorred conflicts that were observed by too many witnesses, but the town had food, lodging, medical facilities, gasoline, communications with the outside world, and even the potential of allies. *It should not be abandoned in haste,* Ivy thought, *for the open road that held mile after mile of Kansas nothing*. He turned down a street that was more commercial and gunned his way down it. Cars were stopped on each side of the boulevard with passengers craning their necks to see the strange weather.

Coming up on a diner attached to a motel called "Cheap Hotel," Ivy pulled the Chevy into a spot hidden from the road. Kelle said, "We should really get out of here."

"Ten blocks or ten miles, that guy won't find us soon, and about now he is meeting the Weyerhaeuser family," Ivy replied.

He looked out of the car. The town center was a riot of storm and clouds, but the chaos seemed contained. It had not followed them.

Kelle seemed about to argue but gave up and pulled a purse from her backpack. "Kelle finally has a Kelly Bag." Like much of what came out of the girl's mouth, this was barely explicable. Ivy waited for Rains-a-Lot to enter the diner, then followed Kelle into it. There was a hat rack near the entrance, and Ivy flung his pork pie on it. His partner kept his hat.

"Never sit in a booth." It was rule nineteen in the *Handbook of Basically Correct and Commonsense Practices for Troubleshooters*. The diner had a few tables near the back with steel and black vinyl chairs. Kelle seemed about to bolt, but Rains-a-Lot forced Kelle into a chair with a grimace. Ivy and he then sat down on either side, all of them facing the entrance.

Rains-a-Lot held up two fingers and brushed his cheek. There were two more exits. He then made a fist with his thumb inserted, held it for a second, and followed that with his two fingers pressing the thumb. The exits were in the bathroom and the kitchen. Ivy rubbed his forehead. That said he understood.

A thin, beady-eyed waitress in a green polyester uniform affixed with her name in script, "Flo," came out and crinkled her nose. "We're not supposed to serve Indians."

Before Ivy could use one of his badges on the woman Kelle said, "My dear, this is my Uncle Don Pablo de Luna, and he happens to be Spanish!"

The waitress squeaked. "Oh, I am so sorry! He's not Mexican?"

"Spanish. Totally different, he is European," she replied.

"Well, I am so sorry, we have to run a clean establishment, you know. What can I get you?" She was glancing at Rains-a-Lot repeatedly.

Kelle pointed at the menu, "Bacon, Lettuce, and Tomato."

The waitress nodded and said, "And you, Don Pablo?"

Ivy answered for Rains-a-Lot, "He wants a grilled steak with grits, and I will have the white bean soup and oven fries."

She wrote down the orders. "Great, anything to drink?"

"Two coffees and two waters." He glanced at Kelle.

"Budwine if you have it." She was smiling, glancing around the restaurant as though it was a museum filled with treasures rather than a greasy spoon in Armpit, Kansas.

The waitress nodded and glanced out the window with apprehension. "The radio said there was an inversion effect, that strange weather was about to hit the county."

Ivy said, "I did not notice." Horizontal rain started to hit the windows with little bits of hail, while wind devils made garbage dance in the parking lot. An umbrella flew by and hit the window with a *thunk*, causing Flo to jump.

Recovering, the waitress finished writing up her ticket and said, "Out in a second."

When she had left earshot, Ivy said, "We are tasked with taking you to a safe location. Before we run out of here, is there anything we need to know?"

Kelle smiled slightly. "That guy is bad news."

"I understand that." The best interrogation technique is often staring, especially when you cannot use copper wire and a blow torch.

Kelle stared back at him then looked over at Rains-a-Lot, obviously herself knowledgeable about the same technique. Their food came to their table steaming in the air conditioning and the air turned suddenly humid. Kelle nervously grabbed her sandwich off the plate. She regarded it for a few seconds and said, "You would think this would be easy to get elsewhen, but in all the times of the world, you have to be in the right space/time to get a real B-L-T sandwich and a bottle of cold Budwine." She bit down on her food with a crunch of lettuce and bacon, the sound filling the silence left by the lack of conversation. "Anyway, that guy is a wizard."

Ivy felt a weight on him as if her words were some sort of physical menace. There was something about lunatics that Dustin-Rhodes seemed to favor and the stranger and crazier they were, the more dangerous they could be. He and Rains-a-Lot had been ordered one time to help some skunk guy in Newberry, South Carolina gather up a load of skunks and deliver them to a ballet school in Rhode Island. The entire way the guy, who was himself somewhat skunk-like in his turnout, could not stop babbling about aliens shaped like bowling balls and intelligent flowers. It was part of the job.

Troubleshooters called them bugs, and it was sad that this woman was infected with that sort of crazy. She was actually pretty in the wan light of the diner, with smooth, clear skin, an intense way of regarding people, and of course, a never-ending font of quips. He had originally thought of her as fifteen, but he was sure now he was a decade off his first estimate. She was fresh-faced and innocent in one light, but in the garish light of bent neon she seemed older, more worldly, perhaps just as worn out as Ivy.

Commenting on wizards though made her a bug, just another task "the Company" assigned to an endless string of terror-filled frivolity and ennui-infected grief. He had about shut down his listening circuits when he caught Rains-a-Lot out of the corner of his eye. The Indian was looking as if he had been beaten by a mullet; he had the sandbagged appearance of someone who forgot their own age and was shocked to find out they were five years older than they had suspected. He reached his hand across the table and touched the Indian's wrist. "Rains, what do you know?"

"The Ghost Dance," he said from between bites of food.

The girl pulled a thick, black-covered, engineer's field notebook and a sleek, stubby pen from her bag. "1890, not too far from here. It was an attempt at a gate combined with a truth rendering, a wisdom service. You have been through a gate?"

The Indian nodded. In their team, it was usually Rains-a-Lot who acted as the silent skeptic, and Ivy took the role of credulity in an interrogation. Strictly speaking, he needed only enough information to deliver their charge to whatever weird science lab she belonged to, and no more. Right now though, they were out of contact with "the Company" and without immediate backup. And of course, being hunted by what had been described as a wizard, a being that was most certainly bullet-proof. Ivy pondered the man who, shot five times, gets back up and rides a lightning bolt into the air. It was his own partner's fatalistic look, though, that made him believe that this was not a scam being run against him. The waitress stalled the conversation by delivering refills for their drinks. Kelle looked at the second Budwine and said in something like a near huge state, "As I said, hard to get, this stuff."

Then, she took out from her purse a ten-dollar bill and said, "Florence, do you have a spare roll of quarters?"

Florence said, "Why sure, dear, I am going to the bank this afternoon, so you can have one of my spare rolls."

"How about two?" Another ten-dollar bill appeared from Kelle's purse.

The waitress took the bills as Kelle started sipping on her bottle of Budwine. She stared at Rains-a-Lot and said, "If you remember the Ghost Dance, then you are over seventy, assuming you were a child when it happened. What year were you born?"

Rains-a-Lot fixed the girl with a spear-like gaze, a lance of intense concentration that Ivy had only seen twice before. "I was born in the year of the White Buffalo."

Ivy said, "Which was?"

"1861," Rains-a-Lot replied.

Florence returned with the coins and the bill. Kelle put the coins in her purse while Ivy, struck dumb by his partner's comment, started to eat from his bowl. He could not remember what he ordered, some type of soup. Kelle seemed to want the conversation to continue. "You could have known Custer!"

Rains-a-Lot looked away.

Ivy nodded fatalistically. Kelle could probably not decode Rains-a-Lot's quiet conversation style, but he just said he was a lot closer related to Custer than just knowing him. Something more was there, and Ivy wished he knew what it was.

Suddenly, Rains-a-Lot was out of his chair. Ivy looked outside and saw that the sky had darkened again and that the parking lot of the Cheap Hotel was filling with pickups, and those trucks were packed to the rim with thugs in jeans and button-down shirts. Ivy threw a handful of money on the table, drew his Browning, and nodded at his partner.

"Told you we had to run," Kelle said. Ivy made sure Kelle had her huge pack, grabbed his pork pie, then pulled her to the bathroom as Rains-a-Lot drew his revolver and left from the front door. As they passed the waitress, Kelle said, "He is letting me practice for the mile-high club." The waitress looked at them as though they had suddenly started speaking Yoruban, but she did not complain at their mutual sudden interest in attending the men's room together.

The bathroom was clean, with a full-sized window on whose eves a small potted daisy had been sat. Ivy slid open the window, ducked out, then back. Kelle grabbed a can of spray cleaner from the counter. "Backpack first," Ivy said. The sound of gunfire started in the distance.

Kelle resisted. "What about your partner?"

Ivy grabbed her pack and threw it out. "He will try not to kill any of them." It was not the answer she was looking for. She stood blinking for a few seconds, then shook it off with a nonplussed look.

Out went the pack, followed by Ivy. He recovered like an Olympic tumbler then reached into the bathroom and pulled Kelle out. She slapped his shoulder and said, "Do not manhandle me."

Ivy ignored her comment and shoved the pack onto her back. "Hold onto my belt," he said. When he had felt her grasp it, he started moving; pistol raised up. He came to the end of the wall leading to the back parking lot when he looked back at Kelle. He put a finger to his lips, and she nodded.

A big meaty face turned the corner and tried to yell, but it was muffled by Ivy putting his Browning in the man's mouth. Ivy said quietly, almost silently, "Anyone behind you?"

The man, his eyes going crossed trying to see the gun, shook his head slightly in the negative.

"I am going to put you to sleep. Better than a nine-millimeter lobotomy, no?" he said.

The man shook his head up and down and murmured, "Yes." Only it came out "roaras" with his mouth around the pistol.

Ivy reached his left hand up and applied pressure to the man's neck. Ten seconds later, he collapsed without a struggle. Kelle asked, "Is it that easy?"

"Either that or he is faking." He looked down at the man. "Waste of a bullet. In either case, he knows what happens if he wakes up."

Ivy started forward, leading them to the corner of the restaurant nearest the Chevy. The purple car was still faced out of a space, windows open. Rain was falling intensely, and the wind was picking up. In the distance, more gunshots and a siren were sounding. Then came an explosion and some screams. Kelle yelped softly, but this understated reaction was calm compared to the chaos in the parking lot.

Ivy motioned to Kelle, indicating the car. She understood and ran for it, throwing her pack and herself in the back seat. Ivy followed her, but halfway to safety, he was blindsided by a 20-stone corn-fed son of Kansas. Taking the hit, he rolled and came to his feet to face a veritable wall of muscle in a Sterling College

Football T-shirt. The young man said, "Gotta fuck you up, sir." Ivy lifted his pistol, but the young man suddenly started leaping and dancing about, patting his ass and screaming. It took a second for Ivy to figure out what had happened. Kelle it seems had emerged from the car and used a lighter and the cleaning spray to burn the poor kid's pants, setting them on fire.

"Put it out before your nuts explode," she said. She threw the can of cleaner and the lighter into the car and grabbed a tiny, flat television set in her hands—the weirdest piece of tech Ivy had ever seen—and some sound started blaring from it like it was a speaker stack. She ducked back into the purple Chevy, and Ivy followed.

Ivy had parked the car in the rear left corner of the restaurant on purpose. He slid into the driver's seat and turned the ignition. The Chevy started with a single crank, and he roared out of the space, then went peeling behind some dumpsters, fishtailing for about twenty meters before throwing the car into a skidding revenue-man's reverse. Right turn, tires squealing and complaining sounds, and they were again in front of the motor lodge. A yellow Packard sedan was burning by the Cheap Hotel's nasty green pool. Four men were rolling on the ground from some form of wound to their legs, courtesy of his partner's preternatural skill with his ancient Smith and Wesson Model 3 revolver. Ivy's head was on a swivel so that he did not miss Rains-a-Lot in the chaos of levitating men, swirling wind, all accompanied by the strange music blasting from the tiny television set Dr. Kelle Brainerd was clutching onto.

The normally reluctant murmur of the car engine had developed into a lion's roar of gas-filled frenzy, as if some deep, personal desire to escape had filled the Chevy's purple metal body. Squishy brakes now reflected the press of Ivy's foot like those of the finest race car, and the wandering tachometer was pegged just under the red as if the engine had decided that nothing but the greatest effort must be given.

Almost too late, Ivy saw Rains-a-Lot detach from a shadow and run for the Chevy's open window. Using both feet, throttling between the gas and brake, Ivy modulated the car's speed and threw it into a skidding slew at the last second to give the Indian the best purchase for entering the vehicle, but Rains-a-Lot hardly needed it. He rocketed through the window into the front seat, allowing Ivy to slam on the gas, punching it through 140 km/h as he hit the open road.

"He is still back there!" Kelle yelled. Her little, flat television was muted for a second but still clutched in her hand.

More than one car was fanning out behind them, but it was an old LaSalle pickup with the strange Wizard standing in it that Kelle was yelling about, and it was gaining on the Chevy with every block. The wind was picking up, and the night had gone from arid and cloudless to heavy and pregnant with rain. In the passenger's seat, Rains-a-Lot had begun to chant:

> A'te he'ye e'yayo! A'te he'ye e'yayo! A'te he'ye lo, A'te he'ye lo. Nitu'fikaflshi'la wa'Tiyegala'ke—kta' e'yayo'! NituTikafishi'la wa' fiyegala'ke—kta' e'yayo'! A'te he'ye lo, A'te he'ye lo. Ni'takuye wanye'giLla'ke—kta e'yayo'! Ni'takuye waflye'gala'ke.

"Arriver comme un cheveu sur la soupe!" Ivy yelled, so scared that his brain was scrubbed of its English, leaving only his birth language.

The wind was growing each second as dust and debris began to slap the Chevy. Ivy closed the passenger window then reached across Rains-a-Lot and awkwardly closed his window as the tip of his foot pressed the gas pedal down. The hurricane blast of air was slowing the Chevy, but somehow was helping the two cars chasing them.

"*Être mal baisé!* This man makes my ass hot!" He forced his brain into English, trying to master his fear while most of his attention kept the slewing car on the road. The Chevy was shaking now with a vibrant fury; rocks were being moved by the fierce wind to batter against the metal skin of the car. Ahead, Ivy saw a vortex cloud blocking the road. *"Merde, merde, merde, Avoir la tête dans le cul!"*

"Drive right into it," Kelle yelled. A new song now played from her tiny, haunted television. It was a song called, "Riders on the Storm."

"*Pisser dans un violon,* no, impossible!" Ivy felt bile in his mouth and thought the top of his skull might split.

A deep purple feeling expanded outward from the roaring heart of the Chevy, embracing the passengers in the warm clasp of motherly love. It was almost like each person was suddenly immersed in a deep deep-lavender bath of comfortably warm oil, pressing down the fear each of them felt and effusing their beings with a strange, preternatural confidence. Ivy felt each other person as an extension of one massive embrace. Violaceous tendrils of hope penetrated deep into each of their squirrel minds and said in a hushed, sultry voice, "Calm, my child, your mother is here." And each felt aware of a gentle tide building and pushing out the rolling panic.

The Chevy grew silent and tomb-like except for the eerie song, while the swirl of dust seemed to move in slow motion before their eyes, the alien purple thoughts settling on each of their minds and allowing them to see each terrible second more clearly. Ivy heard Rains-a-Lot's chanting change to English, calling on the Old Man, the Eagle, the Buffalo, and the Crow to take them to flight and show them bravery, each line matching the haunting beat of the music coming from the little television. He felt Kelle's somatic indignation boil over with anger that she was being crowded by this demonic wizard, his hatred and possessiveness a vile mental dagger stabbing at them all through space, but Ivy was also feeling that purple calm, saying to him with purple footsteps like the silken tones of a woman speaking gently accented French, "Take to the center of the storm and believe in the gateway."

The car bucked in slow motion while the freight train of wind gently batted it around second by second. At the edge of his being, Ivy felt a terrible clawing, a caterwaul of anger, the voice of the Wizard demanding that he stop his car and surrender Kelle to him. Then, he felt a reply from Kelle; her middle finger forcefully pumped at the magician, though this was only a mental construct. Her defiance caused the Wizard's anger to explode across the entire landscape of Ivy's mind, and he was proud of the diminutive woman who was like the lion's prey telling the lion to fuck himself seconds before he closed his jaws on her being. How can you not love that bravura defiance at the edge of a storm?

Then, he saw a point in the maelstrom that glowed a beautiful yellow light. It was a place that transcended dimension and plane, a place whose existence was causing a rip in two worlds, feeding the awful power of the wind. Kelle said, "There is a convergence here, and the Wizard cannot control his creation, not as he wants." A purple thought in the middle of his brain agreed and urged Ivy forward into the maw of cataclysm.

Ivy accelerated at the center of the storm, his mind half-sure that this was a death move. Who could survive driving into the middle of a Kansas tornado?

They crashed through to the other side and were immediately traveling more than 100 km/h down a packed dirt road in a snow-covered landscape. Just as the car's wheels had bitten into the ground, they began to plow through a formation of people dressed in steel armor, running over at least 200 of the soldiers before Ivy could finally brake the Chevy to a barely controlled stop in front of a huge warrior in a bear hat. This man immediately brought an iron flail down on the car's hood, which caused the Chevy to accelerate again without Ivy pressing the pedal down, seemingly of its own volition, crushing the final knight beneath the car's wheels and grinding his chest to a pulp.

Kelle unbuckled her seat belt and looked around both at the fleeing soldiers and at a smaller and more pathetic army of poorly dressed peasants who were armed with pitchforks and rusty glaives. "We are not in Kansas anymore," she announced.

Rains-a-Lot replied stiffly, "No shit, Dorothy."

MIND GAMES WITH DARTS

DATE: NOVEMBER 24, 2017
LOCATION: PETERBOROUGH, NEW HAMPSHIRE

I hit <Command><S> on my computer right after I write the words, "No shit, Dorothy," surprised that the normally taciturn Rains-a-Lot would make such a popular cultural reference. Pinned on my corkboard is the letter from my neurologist, recapping that wonderful diagnosis meeting where five medical doctors told me I am screwed in scientific language, though they did so with kind hearts.

A bottle of Valproate sits on my computer desk. For nearly twenty years, it has been all that stood between me and the senile dementia brought on by epileptic seizures. Three months ago, my insurance agency, concerned with ever-changing regulations coming out of Washington D.C., and the eventual demise of the Affordable Care Act, had required that I change my medication to a cheaper drug called Lamotrigine. The result was a near-fatal bout of Stephens-Johnson syndrome, which was controlled only at the last minute by an experimental and risky therapy.

I pick up my walking stick, which I had named Grandfather. It is about my height, with the face of an old man apparent in the cracks of the wood. Near the end, in the hospital, somehow the stick had shown up by my bed. It remained there throughout my illness, watching over me as I slept, as nurses and doctors fought to revive me from cardiac arrest, and as the experimental therapy was jammed into my veins while nervous medics fought to keep the IV machines from shutting down because of the breakneck pace I was being dosed. When I finally awoke alive, there was my old bottle of Valproate waiting for me and a walking stick that the hospital avowed had not allowed into intensive care.

When I had taken Valproate for a few days, though, the doctors discovered an unsettling fact. It did not have its original effectiveness at treating epilepsy. The seizures had slowly returned. And with the seizures came the likelihood of dementia and death. The doctors rapidly tested other drugs, but it was always the same. I could not tolerate them, they had no effect, or they would trigger the deadly and fearsome Stephens-Johnson syndrome, an allergic reaction that caused the patient's body to reject his skin, simulating third-degree burns and painful, lingering death.

At the diagnostic meeting, I asked, "How long do I have?"

The room had grown quiet. It stayed that way for a second while each medical practitioner considered, staring at the walls then glancing at their colleagues. Finally, the lead resident said, "That question is very hard to answer. There is no firm line between your current mental state and the mental state where you will consider your quality of life to be severely affected, negatively so. Each time you have an epileptic seizure, it will likely take something from you, some bit of intellect. It could be a year, though, before it takes enough that you can tell you are declining. Or it could take your vision, your hearing, or your motor functions tomorrow. We simply do not know. Think of your mentality as a dartboard and epilepsy like a drunken dart player. There is no telling where the dart will fall, but eventually, the board will be full of darts."

Ironically, I could still drive. Epilepsy patients who had distinct auras as I did could drive because they had clear warnings of their epilepsy minutes before the seizure struck. I was not allowed to drive in heavy traffic, like Los Angeles, or over long bridges or tunnels. It was an hour back from Dartmouth-Hitchcock Medical Center to Peterborough where my writing offices and apartment were, and I drove like a zombie.

It was not that I would die. Death was a constant companion of mine because of events in my past that could never be undone. I dreamed of fields of burning soybeans. I remembered colleagues, friends, and lovers who had died trying to accomplish things that made them heroes in my heart. I was a creative consultant. I no longer accomplished things; I just smoothed the path for others to make a difference in the creative world. Maybe it was better I die than some artist who was fighting poverty and ridicule to bring something new into the world. Still, the idea I would be sliding into senility scared me. My mind had always been my most important element of my being.

That night, I purchased two bottles of La Vieille Ferme Côtes du Ventoux red, the writer's tonic, and a new Winmau dartboard. I printed out a picture of the human brain and held a lonely game of drunken darts. I would drink a glass of wine, then throw darts at the color print of the brain pinned to the board. As I got drunk, the darts started to hit all over the board with soft thunks, and I could smell the wafting odor of new dartboard cork. Eventually, the standard deviation of the throws grew to include the bookshelves on either side of the board. Each time a dart went into the board, I would recover it, place a little orange target dot on the place where it hit, then return to throwing. I ran out of wine and started in on the filing cabinet that contained my stronger medicinals.

Two bottles in, plus seven glasses of Bénédictine and nine cans of Boag's Beer (a leftover from this year's author's party), and the brain picture was a solid mass of orange. There was one last sip in the last open Bénédictine bottle and two more darts. I sipped the brandy, more of a gulp, then threw the first of the remaining missiles.

A bullseye. The Kenyan sisal the board was constructed of caused the dart to vibrate madly as it hung in the middle of the bullseye. Good stuff, Kenyan sisal.

And that's about it. I do not imagine God as the dart thrower. He or She is more likely the bartender. Heaven, I imagine, is a bar like the old Jim Collins I used to go to in Savannah, back when I was young enough to hitchhike across Mexico and not think it was a feat worth reporting to my friends. No, I imagined the dart thrower was the shade of Chekov. And here I meant Anton, not Pavel Andreievich, and his darts were fired from an impressive hand crossbow made of silver and heartwood. Only like me, he is drunk. But unlike me, God lets him drink on the house. The best I can do is happy hour if I bring a date and let her order.

One last dart. I really had to pee, so I threw it as hard as I could. So far the darts had only caused minor damage to a copy of one of my books when they missed the target and flew randomly across the room. Most of the other books were sufficiently agile enough to dodge poorly thrown missiles, likely having used various tricky ways to buff their armor class when they saw the arrival of a dartboard and a metric shitload of alcohol.

I could hear the stricken book totter on the shelf, giving the whole death scene a real Hollywood finish. After a few seconds of creaking elegy, it fell to the floor in a swan-mush of flapping pages and cracking bindings. Holding my bladder with Herculean force—there should be medals for things like not peeing your pants after an epic drunk—I turned and grabbed the book. It was *The Wonderful Wizard of Oz* by L. Frank Baum. It had to be that book. I had never read it.

Clutching the tome to my chest, I tacked like a sailing craft plying against the wind to my bathroom. The trick to drunk peeing is to catch the crafty porcelain bowl in a position of enfilade before you set your internal gyros to compensate for the swaying of the deck below your feet. If you do this, then you have a nice, long target to pee into and a high chance that the entire salvo will at least bracket your target, if not score direct hits.

Lining myself up with great confidence, I decided that the issue of urination was well in hand, and I could consider my long connection to the fable. In 1986, I had, through a series of misadventures, visited a communist intellectual debate camp in the deserts of Mexico above the town of Matamoros. The camp was for college students of distinctly left-wing interests, taught by college professors of an equally slanted worldview—it even had communal showers. It was those showers that had drawn me to the place since I was a high school dropout, a Quaker, rather right-wing in my economic views, and definitely a believer in the system of democratic republics. However, I was willing to listen to indoctrination if I got to shower with college-aged women.

Anyhow, during one of my few collisions with drugs, a professor handed out doses of Mescaline and then lectured on Quetzalcoatl. It was a great lecture although my hearing was troubled by a distinct copper smell, and as he described an alternate universe that existed, I made a joke to a dark-haired, beautiful Mexican college student about this being more like a discussion of the land of Oz. The professor stopped the lecture and said, "You of all people, Comrade Nelson, should not joke about Oz."

I finished peeing and reached out to flush, but the toilet had moved more than a meter to my left. That required a tricky extension to reach the handle, one that I proudly completed. Turning to leave, I almost fell; a pipe must have had a small leak because the floor was wet, and my house shoes were not all-terrain. Holding the book above my head as I saw Marines do, crossing Alligator Creek in the Battle of Guadalcanal, I waded to dry land and began the northern tack that would take me safely past Savo Island to my reading chair.

I aimed for my chair but wound up on my bed. The doctors said it was impossible to tell when epilepsy had first struck me. I knew, though. It was in a field in Iowa when a giant plane came crashing down near me in 1989. The bodies, the smells, the feeling of slipping into another world, and I was in a special place. A dreamland where airliners did not fall from the heavens on sunny August days.

That dreamland was a place of magic. I was only a bird, but I could fly anywhere, see anything, and understand a lot more than a bird should. I met the Spider Queen who spun her webs across Virdea. I saw the Yellow King build a tyranny across the lowlands while his brother, the Fell Wizard of the Great Obsidian Tower, connived for power in the Delta. I saw on her throne the Queen of Fire and Ice in the great city of Emeralds, and the Pirate of the Batterseas on top of her great ships of wood. It was a land of wonder that just happened to look a lot like the world we live in.

There were thousands of stories in Virdea. The story of the Mulberry Priestess, the song of the Vine Tore Warrior, the book of Silence, and the epic of the Four all would flash before me as I flew across the land. There were strange moments of clarity, though. I saw a purple 1957 Chevy standing in front of the gate to the Green City with a clear view of its black-rimmed, white-colored license plate with the number 60-9866 stamped on it. A modern Iowa license.

I woke up the next morning with a headache and a lot of cleaning to do. I had written down "Iowa 1960 60-9866" in Sharpie on the bottom of my worktable along with the words "Get to Work."

The yearly epileptic seizures of my youth became monthly in my middle twenties, then weekly in my thirties, and Virdea became a part-time home as my health declined. Then, the doctors eventually found a way to beat them back, and I had forgotten Virdea as a hallucination controlled by Valproate. Now, the seizures were back, and my own drunk self had just told the somber me to get to work.

It made perfect sense in a twisted way. The doctors said I could live twenty or thirty more years, but my intellectual self was sitting under the sword of Damocles. Next week, or next year, when the string snaps, I will become an interesting form of houseplant. I have no desire to commit seppuku—that falls to someone with the theatrical talent of Masayuki Mori, not to the likes of me. Instead, I have decided to work as fast and as hard as I can to tell the story of how a 1957 Chevy could end up in Virdea.

Research has always been easy for me. Although it had been epilepsy that robbed me of my chance of earning a Ph. D. I had completed my dissertation and came damn close to defending it. I would forever be considered ABD, which means "All But Dissertation," at South Carolina, but the rules said I could never complete the degree. Despite this, great scholars like Dr. Lynn Zeller and Dr. Eric Coggins taught me to be a critical thinker and a strong researcher and nothing could take that away from me.

I laughed. Something would take it away from me, but for now, I have it, so I will use it.

Research really boils down to finding someone who knows more than you do and asking them the right questions to separate the subjective from objective. A license plate was easy. Bail Cannon who had a weird hobby of automotive records kept an amazing database of state and national vehicle records. He actually helped solve cold cases, filled in holes in the national vehicle database, and was forever being used by rare automobile experts to answer tiny questions about vehicles. I shot him an e-mail.

To: CannonB
From: McKeebyN
RE: Iowa 1960 60-9866
Date: 12 November 2017

Contents: Bail, tell me anything you can on the automobile assigned this plate. Bill me what I owe you.

In just an hour, I had an answer.

To: McKeebyN
From: CannonB
RE: Iowa 1960 60-9866
Date: 12 November 2017

Contents: Nelson, registered to Dustin-Rhodes Corporation of 406 Sixth Avenue, Des Moines, Iowa. 1957 Chevy. Vehicle acquired December, 1957, and amortized as total loss August, 1960. Cause listed, weather. Insurance form says its loss was at or near Bashful, Kansas.

The Internet is amazing, but so is the idea, proven here that no matter how obscure, modern society will have an expert at anything you seek to know. I wrote an info card for the 1957 Chevy and put it on my cork board, then printed the e-mail, and put it into my paper files.

Bashful, Kansas was harder to find. Here is a strange fact: there are thousands of ghost towns across the United States. Each year, hundreds of towns cease to exist in any record save historical as their last citizens die, the community goes bankrupt, global warming causes it to slide into the ocean or burn up in desert heat, or it simply slips from memory.

My parents were busy folks who did many wonderful things, but near the end of their lives, they took the last of their meager savings and bought a tiny house in the wilderness of Northern Florida near a town called Two Egg. I am not sure why they chose this to be the place of their last stand, but within a year they had both died of cancer (or maybe they died together because they had no other idea of a happy life without the other). I drove through the place a couple of years later and saw a community with a great deal of pride and love holding onto a name as hard as they could, but always knowing that it was a losing battle. Near the corner of Florida 69 and Florida 69A, someone had put up a sign that said, "Remember Us, Two Egg." I asked about the sign at a small insurance agency, and no one knew who put it there. As I said goodbye to my parents, I thought of that sign. I had been the one who had paid for its construction and then had slipped out of responsibility by pointing it out and asking who else had been the one who had built it.

Bashful was a town that weather destroyed, but unlike Two Egg, no one had ever bothered to put up a sign to mark its passing. It is a strange thing, but on the Internet of Everything, not everything exists. Instead, you have to dig deeper into things that exist in strange corners of the human collective mind. For me, small libraries attached to colleges and universities are the perfect place for local research. Being a student at a place with 90,000 books and no LexisNexis is hard, but those libraries act as vacuum cleaners of knowledge, scooping up defunct meeting notes, police records, newspaper galleys, and everything else that modern society has cut loose in its efforts to nationalize and modernize. I called Wabash and got a student worker.

"This is Nelson Mckeeby, I am working on the Virdea project." The fact that I had not named this project yet was off the subject. It was now the Virdea project. The book would be named whatever it ended up being named.

"Bell Selshy, sir." It was a young woman on the phone, sounding eager and happy to talk.

I put on my professorial hat, "Do you know how to use your database to find local records, Ms. Selshy?"

"Yes, sir!" I could hear the exclamation points in her voice.

I took a few notes then asked, "Do you have time to get me whatever you have on Bashful?"

She almost yelped. "My grandparents went to Bashful High School. I mean, before the thing, you know."

"What thing?" I asked.

Her voice grew hushed. "The inversion."

"What was that?" I hastily scribbled down the word "inversion" on a notepad.

"A giant tornado destroyed the town. It was never built again. My dad said it was like the tornado reached down into the history books and scraped the town off the very pages of our textbooks." She sounded flustered like it was hard to recall such a huge event.

"Really?" I said.

She hesitated. "Sure. You can drive through Bashful, but it is not even a ghost town. It is gone for good."

"You are a treasure; can I arrange to interview you or your parents?" This was the true importance of the call, finding someone to get me information on the last days of the town of Bashful. I looked at my pad and found I had been drawing an image of a man in a suit with a smoking head. I laughed and erased it.

Something broke loose with her hesitation. "Yes, and I can copy the Bashful file for you. Do you have an account?"

I made a research account with the library and ended up getting a box full of photocopies. Plus, I got three interviews with the Selshy family members that remembered Bashful as a bonus. Her grandmother Flo even remembered the events of the day the town was leveled.

The book had begun in earnest.

THE ENCHANTED GUITAR

DATE: DECEMBER 19, 1964
LOCATION: PUERTO VALLARTA, MEXICO

As an author, sometimes I have to drop into first person to explain things to my readers, a habit that gave my writing instructors fits. You see, only classical writers can do strange things like shifting tense or changing the timing of what they write. Mundane writers who do not fit the mold of what a writer should be must stick to the narrative version of iambic pentameter and behave themselves so as not to get a bad grade on a creative writing paper, which, given the state of technology, is two lies and a half-truth in one phrase.

Here is an example of what made my teachers crazy. Sometimes I need to introduce characters to people before they ever enter the main story. Way before. Which means, much to the chagrin of some of the characters in the book already introduced, they all have to be parked on a siding, waiting to be picked up again and their story continued.

So Dr. Kelle Brainerd, Rains-a-Lot, Ivy d'Seille, and an unusual purple 1957 Chevy are sitting in a land called Virdea after having killed the great king of that magical land and plowed through his soldiers, turning many into a disgusting, pink paste. And the researcher/author of that scene is preparing for an epileptic seizure that will send him to that same magical land. Meanwhile, that same author, me, is writing a drawn-out forward to a chapter about another character who will matter later in these books but is not yet known. Robert Anton Wilson and Robert Joseph Shea had a notable advantage over the author in that they had acid trips, while the author only has terminal status epilepsy and a skin disease called TEN (Toxic Epidermal Necrolysis) from the medication that could save his mind.

Anyway, in an era when simple sells, this is a lot of complexity. So why do it?

Ask Terasaka Kichiemon why he needed 47 ronin to tell his story. Well, that is a bad example because it is a historical tale ... and there were 47 ronin. Or perhaps that is a good example because the real world is not about one hero and 46 extras, but 47 heroes of their own story.

So open up your browser and go to Google Maps. Enter in the coordinates 20° 38′ 45″ N, 105° 13′ 20″ W. Zoom in until you see Francisco Medina Ascencio, a road that runs through town. Look for Playa Las Glorias, and you will find a beach where a young man sits. I mean, he is sitting there in 1964 before all the hotels and resorts have been built. The young man has just bought a guitar from a store in Fluvial Vallarta and has come to the beach to look at it and try it out.

The guitar is magical. I do not mean in the mundane sense of being nice and alluring, but in the real pipe-hitting, pointy hat, wand-waving sense that it can do things that other guitars cannot.

Meet Randolph Homey.

Randolph Homey sits on the beach holding his new guitar. It was an amazing instrument. A real Ramirez—much better constructed than a ukulele or a practice guitar at school. The instrument held endless potential. His biggest thought at that second (in 1964) was the worry that he would never learn the nuances of playing it.

That single thought may cause the reader of this work, who has newly acquired it in some ancient bookstore from a stack of similar works, to smile. This is because you, the reader, are living in the twenty-first century and probably have heard of Randolph Homey, or at least of his musical group, the Portals. Unless you are living in a yurt, and psychographic tests of this book showed yurt-dwellers were unlikely to go in for magical realism (which is pretty strange when you think of it), then you have heard Randolph Homey's music in advertisements, as the soundtracks in movies, and even as iTunes downloads. Heck, you might have even bought a record by the band if your memory extends that far back.

Of course, Randolph Homey never was the most famous member of the Portals. That distinction would have to go to Jack Rovane, the beat poet whose stage presence, sex appeal, and belief in performance art dominated the covers of major media outlets. You will get to meet Rovane later. Right now, it is Homey's turn.

If you know of the Portals, then likely you know of them from a series of movies produced by directors with Oliver Stone complexes. That is ... the guys who never knew a great, true-to-life story, they could not muck up with an hour of conspiracy-theory-driven exposition. Which might mean this book will be the first place where you will finally learn the truth of this amazing band and their mission to save the world. However, at this second, it is just Randolph Homey and a flamenco guitar. And that guitar is magical. Holding the guitar he says, "I hope I can learn to be a great musician."

"You will." It was an otherworldly voice answering the call of a young man.

He nodded. If his inner voice had said he would be a good guitarist, then it was like a type of destiny. He began to strum the strings with his fingers and was delighted at the sonorous output. He thought of a pick as he felt how even playing a short while rubbed the skin raw.

The voice said, "The pick stands in the way of the magic."

Randolph agreed with himself. His inner voice was dark, deep, black. Not like some evil forbidding shadow cast to intimidate, but like the warm darkness of midnight that embraces you when you start to fall asleep in a safe bed where you can trust everything around you.

"Keep going, Randolph." His internal voice, the soft darkness, folded in on him. He played intensely for five minutes, then looked up. Gone was the beach. Gone was the tourist town with its edgy slums. Instead, Randolph was face-to-face with a bright woman in fiery red and crystalline blue. She clapped her hands and said, "Welcome to Virdea."

The beach is gone. The sun is dimmer. The weather is colder. The land is now green rather than golden. And there is a strange castle on the rise.

A woman in a shimmering robe approaches. "The talisman shares my greetings, welcome to Virdea."

"Wow," Randolph says.

"I am sure you have a million questions for me and the talisman," the woman said.

Randolph stood up, guitar in one hand, and brushed sand from his Bermuda shorts with the other. "No, I get it. This is a magical land like Oz, and the guitar brought me here to offer me a chance to learn music and become a troubadour. I read the whole Oz thing, so of course, this is neat!"

The guitar laughed, and the woman looked a little crestfallen. "What a shame. I am quite good at exposition. This is not Oz though. Oz is a place where you wake up after a thirty-day debauch to find you have signed on as an oiler on a freighter. It is called Australia in more mundane terms, and other than having horrible creatures that are always trying to kill you, Virdea is a much different place."

"Not a problem. Do you have something warmer to wear while we get to my training?" Randolph asked.

The guitar said, "I never favored those Nathaniel Coxon knickers people wear."

The woman sighed. "My name is Jessica, and the talisman is known as Guitar."

"You mean this guitar is named Guitar?" Randolph said.

Jessica sighed. "My princess, the Lady of Fire and Ice, is seeking the smart, the strong, the ethical, and the creative to fill her court. Virdea is a place where causality and correlation can be reversed at times, and she is seeking a counter to the hands of deceptive people who would poison our lands. And that is the offer. If you wish to learn to play, you have to aid us in our efforts. Come to court and inspire our people to resist the darkness."

At this point, the readers know enough about Randolph and his relation to the magical land of Virdea so that they will not be confused when he shows up later in the stories.

CASE ORANGE

DATE: AUGUST 9, 1960
LOCATION: DES MOINES, IOWA

Dustin-Rhodes was a giant company. The CEO, Richard Todd Hamblin, a fan of *Seven Brides for Seven Brothers*, had required his seven assistants to legally change their names to Adam, Benjamin, Caleb, Daniel, Ephraim, Frank, and Gideon. The seven white men had complied because the benefits of the position were so damn good, and at least the big man had not taken a liking to *One Thousand and One Nights*. When the big man was angry, he would threaten to start hiring new assistants, starting with Milly. So far the threat had been hollow.

The one thing that each of the senior executive vice presidents noted was their boss's complete inability to consider any subject brought to his attention as frivolous and his total willingness to forgive anything but a complete fabrication. At the Executive Vice President's (EVP) Club on the thirty-ninth floor of the Grand Building, located inconveniently in the city of Des Moines, Iowa, each of the men would wonder what would happen if a giant lizard attacked the city of Gulfport, Florida (where the big man kept his summer house). The common agreement was that he would order the person informing him of the potential destruction of Webb City, his favorite store, and the possible movement of the lizard toward his favorite restaurant, a small Greek joint on the Tarpon Springs sponge docks, to have a couple of Troubleshooters borrow a Thunderchief fresh from the production lines and "take care of it." This would be followed directly by an order to short Republic stock and an announcement for a plan for Fairchild to take Republic over. Of course, that did not mean the big man had no vanity. At some point, he would jot out a small note to send to his archenemy, Alexander P. de Seversky, with a burnt half-copy of the book *Victory Through Air Power* that said simply, "FUCK YOU ALEX, I JUST FUCKED YOUR COMPANY AGAIN."

There was no doubt the big man was a genius. The oldest surviving EVP remembered leaving a note from a Troubleshooter written on the back of a page from the *CRC Handbook of Chemistry and Physics*. Ignoring the note, the big man had instead made corrections to a math problem on the reverse side and handed it back, saying, "Send this over to that guy at Convair, you know, the guy that did my taxes last year." There turned out to be endless talk over the corrected problem. The old man made history with his answer to a single math problem.

So when Benjamin Day, whose name had ironically been Caleb before the great name change in 1954, brought a single note to the big man, it was no surprise that their great leader did not need to look into his huge filing cabinets for information on its meaning. What was surprising was the resulting emotional outburst. Richard Todd Hamblin, who had only been known to show emotions outwardly twice (when Franklin Delano Roosevelt died and when John Fitzgerald Kennedy was nominated, each time proclaiming that the human species needed to develop some form of immortality for "special people") began to scream at the top of his lungs and curse in a language that the secretaries were later able to determine was Portuguese.

Standing in the withering fire of romance-language expletives, Benjamin Day thought of his own work that year with the three-colored retirement system. Green retirements offered the loyal and hardworking employees of Dustin-Rhodes health care, a monthly stipend, access to the Hot Springs, North Carolina spa, along with attractive discounts to certain restaurants in Mars Hill, and low-cost season tickets to games played by the new American Football League (who had received a sweetheart deal with Dustin-Rhodes in exchange for expanding the league to Florida in the next eight years).

The blue retirement was not as nice. Basically, a blue retirement meant that you were given a name change, a straw hat, and a hut in the bustling metropolis of Komuvaha, along with a retirement income tending the small shrine to the big man's departed son, Lester, a few miles north of town. There were other variants of this theme, but they all consisted of living on an island in a hut in the southern hemisphere, cutting away crabgrass from some small piece of earth where a memorial to a dead kid was left.

The red retirement was the one that Benjamin Day had been most excited about. The retiree would be honored by a bagpipe procession, a donation of several thousand dollars in their honor to one of a number of private colleges in the southern United States, and the naming of an asteroid after them. The retiree also would get an exciting retirement home in a beautiful community in Millidgeville, Georgia that consisted of an eight-by-four plot of ground, a wooden "Grand Caesar" six-pole internment box with satin interior work and brass fittings, and the choice of a Baptist or Catholic service performed by a trained liturgist.

Suddenly, Benjamin Day saw that all of his hard work could backfire completely. And the only way his life would be saved was to immediately determine, or better, anticipate, the big man's needs and wishes, and see that they were met very quickly.

Sustaining the verbal abuse, Benjamin Day stepped to the door and wrote a short note to the secretary. It said:

ITEM ONE: Translator

ITEM TWO: File for action Able 70

ITEM THREE: Activate war room

ITEM FOUR: Deliver (1) case TastyKake Butterscotch Krimpet

ITEM FIVE: Deliver (1) case Budwine

ITEM SIX: Activate employee Devine, Delbert

The first translator that arrived was for Catalonian but was quickly replaced by a person fluent in Brazilian

Portuguese, although it turned out most of the translation was cursing. Day was amazed that the Portuguese language consisted mostly of different ways of saying "vagina" and sent the translator away.

By the time the big man had slowed his cursing, the file from the war room was in Day's hands. It said in the cryptic computerese of the giant machines that filled an entire Iowa office building on Tenth Street:

> "Troubleshooter TEAM GULF (d'Seille / Smith) to collect asset A70 (Brainerd94) and deliver to secure facility Wyoming03 Condition Bravo."

Thinking ahead, Benjamin Day wrote on an action item slip, "86 employee d'Seille, 86 employee Smith," and he handed it to a courier.

"Who was the person responsible for picking up Brainerd?" the big man finally asked.

Day was, by default, the only person who would funnel data to the big man. It was how things worked. "Agent d'Seille and Agent Smith, Troubleshooter team Gulf."

Richard Todd Hamblin waived his hand. "Reliable men, perfectly able to handle things."

Benjamin Day wrote two more slips, "Cancel 86 employee d'Seille" and "Cancel 86 employee Smith," and handed them to the courier. The big man walked back and forth for a minute while Able fretted before two slips returned: "86 cancel confirmed employee Smith" and "86 carried out d'Seille." The door to the room swung open, and Benjamin Day saw a crowd of people around one of the steno girls who was bleeding out on the floor from a head wound. Taking another slip, he wrote:

"Request 05 on recent action, 86 d'Seille."

The reply came back very quickly.

"05: 86 carried out on d'Seille, Doris, Grade STENO 2, Des Moines Offices, floor 13."

He shrugged and jotted off a note to compliment Human Resources on its rapid response to his requests. Then he heard the big man say, "This is Case ORANGE."

Everything changed forever at that moment.

THE GIRL IN THE CLOSET

DATE: JUNE 9, 2012
LOCATION: NEW YORK CITY, NEW YORK

The space she considered her room was about seven feet by three feet and lined with cedar. In her mind, she knew she could claim the bedroom outside the closet as hers, or the entire floor of the tower she lived in, far above the bustle of the ant heap that was New York. Since her mother went away, though, she had made a conscious choice to narrow the dimensions of what was hers.

The closet was hers and no one interfered as she modified it for her needs. Kelle had found a daybed in the outer apartment and had pushed it into her space. A fire extinguisher was grabbed from the kitchenette because she was aware of safety. Using some tools left by a worker in the dayroom, she had installed it with some brackets. She had broken out the wall and shoved the front of her computer in along with two monitors. They looked untidy from the living room where they plugged into the Internet and power, but they made a nice place to study and do computer work. Her closet was all cedar, nice-smelling and well-built, so she had been careful to make a small eating place near the front and refrained from make meals anywhere else to avoid crumbs.

In a nook, she had placed a picture of her mother. The only picture she had.

Mom existed, somewhere. For ten years, she had not returned, and nothing she did would entice her staff to communicate with her. Security arranged no visits. There were no letters or cards from her, and none could be sent. No presents came at Christmas, and no one offered to carry her presents in return. Mom had gone from a crying presence—sobbing softly in the sewing room over issues of Vanity Fair—to a hole in existence.

It was only in the last year that she started to feel it might have been her own fault. Ten years ago, her mother had left in the night after a terrible row with her father. Then, the next month, her father had come to her in the night sobbing, seeking some sort of absolution for something he did. Kelle looked at him as he cried and could not bring herself to talk. She should have. If she had used that little window in time, she could have negotiated for her mother's return, but she had stood stupid and mute. He had never come again, and she never had a chance in all those years to beg her father for her mother to return. Father and daughter now communicated only through notes, although she understood that he had a daily report on her activities. The staff told her this, and they had no reason to lie.

Kelle had an endless expense account. If she had wanted, Aloïs would have taken her shopping each day. No one would care. She could eat herself into obesity, never wear the same clothing twice, and let herself go stark. Aloïs was not provided to protect her from herself. He was there to prevent her from being harmed or bringing shame on her father or his company. Kelle only knew where the limit of Aloïs's duties lay by testing them and had failed to find those edges repeatedly. If she asked Aloïs to parachute off the balcony, he would have made a safe set of equipment and instructors to see her to the ground, and he would have been waiting to collect her and take her back to the apartment and the safety of her closet.

She had been eight when she asked Aloïs if he would purchase her drugs. "I am not instructed to not do this." His answers to questions were often configured to force her to decide for herself if the question was appropriate. Her father thus did not care if she took drugs, but Aloïs would have disapproved.

At eight years old, Kelle knew she had a pretty good grasp on the world and sat down to think if she really wanted drugs. She had seen a documentary on them and wondered what it would feel like to just take them and go to sleep. She had sat at the computer in her closet looking at different drugs and reading what they did. She studied the lingo of drug use, watched videos on how they affected the brain, and looked at statistics of who took what drugs. In the end, she did not ask Aloïs again for drugs.

Aloïs was brilliant. He spoke eight languages and used to protect the children of Middle Eastern dictators. Kelle was in love with him because he was the only person who talked to her instead of at her or about her.

"So, you would get me drugs?" she asked with a furtive, wheedling tone. She had already decided against taking them, but now the issue was seeing how far she could push the limits of her world.

Aloïs had the driver pull over the rig that she called Monster and said, "Does the Miss want drugs?"

She made a serious face and said, "Maybe."

Her protector looked seriously at her. "Perhaps the Miss would listen to a servant who perhaps understands what she asks."

She thought for a second, then said, "Maybe." Then she said, "I know all about drugs. I am not a child. I will be nine next month. I learned all there is to know about drugs."

"The Miss read her first book when she was two years old," Aloïs replied. "Nothing that the Miss wants to know is beyond her grasp." He leaned forward and removed a spot of dirt from her blouse. A tiny, endearing gesture. "You have already decided you do not want drugs. This is a test the Miss is setting up for her servant Aloïs."

"How do you know this?" she asked.

Aloïs rolled his eyes. It was their private code for the secret things that floated about her life like clouds. It meant Aloïs felt she was smart enough to do sums without the handholding she needed when she was younger. Eight-year-olds should know the ways of the world.

She said definitively, "I am good at reading."

"Why not read some more books on drugs, and then next year, if you still want some, we will arrange a supply for you." And she knew he meant it. He never said things like that if he was unwilling to pay up. "You read many books, but perhaps not enough, and I suspect you already decided on this issue, but have not informed Aloïs of the real answer."

Aloïs was very wise, it turned out. After a few weeks more of reading, she admitted that it was not even a good test of Aloïs's loyalty to her to have him buy drugs. Then she turned nine and realized that she was smarter than eight, and there was no reason at all to even consider drugs.

Kelle had instead purchased a JanSport D2 pack and said to herself, "This is home." She began to stock the pack with everything she would need to survive on her own outside of the apartment. One day though, she came into the bedroom, and the pack was gone. She asked one of the maids where it was, and the man said, "You do not need that thing, and it keeps us from cleaning."

She screamed at the maid and ran into her closet.

Aloïs found her sitting in the closet, so he entered and kneeled down. "Young Miss, you yelled at the maids?"

"You do not miss much, Aloïs." She laughed at the idea of an adult male crouching in a closet with her.

He smiled, "I am quite observant."

"A regular Doctor House," she replied.

"Who?" he asked.

She had to bridge the communication gap. "Sherlock Holmes," she suggested as a stand-in.

Aloïs chuckled, "British? No, young Miss, consider me more like C. Auguste Dupin. I am not homophobic, but Master Holmes is a little closer to Watson than would be my comfort."

"Then Dupin. And yes, I am sleeping in a cedar closet. Been doing that for three years. Nice of you to notice." Aloïs always understood and respected her statements of fact.

"Interesting." They sat in silence for a minute.

"No one cares if I sleep in a closet," she said.

He patted her shoulder and said, "As you say."

Silence for another minute.

"Do they?" she asked.

Aloïs shifted. "You generated a thirty-one-page report from this." He stopped for a second, then said, "And another twenty-page report on the backpack and your reaction to it being taken."

"In an hour?" She was amazed that so much could be written about what would be, at most, a single line in the book of her life.

He laughed his deep laugh. "Several people contributed to the report."

"Did you?" she asked.

"I confirmed you were sitting in the closet and that your backpack had been taken," he responded.

Silence.

She looked at Aloïs's passive face, his angular jawline, and his perfectly pressed suit. "You are doing it again."

"What is that, young Miss?" he asked.

"Interrogating me." She crossed her arms across her chest.

He nodded sagely. "Yes, young Miss, it is as you say."

More silence.

"I want to know what is mine." She was starting to cry.

Aloïs nodded. "Of course, Miss."

"Is this closet mine?" she asked, tears streaking her cheeks.

Aloïs rolled his eyes.

She sobbed harder. "The backpack?"

He kicked the wall gently with his toe. "Does that huge thing mean anything to you? Does this closet matter?"

She looked at her security guard with contempt, then modified her face to show respect. Then she cried even harder.

He surprised her by saying, "Then, it is yours; you can leave with it on your back. The maids will be instructed to return it and never touch it again."

"What if I did leave? What if I took my pack and moved to Madison County, North Carolina?" She was sure the answer was she was a prisoner.

Aloïs again surprised her. "If you did leave of your own will and in a way that prevented you from becoming an issue for your father and the corporation, it would provide work for many report writers, and my security detail would have to find a way to protect you in the field. Even in this place called Madison County. Is there such a place? I must begin to prepare."

She thought this over. An hour later the pack, with all of her treasure untouched, was returned.

Again she had to test the idea. She placed the pack in the way of the maids. She set it up as a pitfall. She hid it behind things and under things. It was never touched again, and she forgot about Madison County.

Years passed. The man whom she thought of as her true father taught her many lessons, but time withers all things and, by corporate policy, he was retired before his pension could become a burden on the company. Others took his place as she conquered the sciences, published papers, and was awarded degrees. She kept the pack but soon left the closet for her normal room, and the oddities of her youth passed by as the years did.

She was seventeen now, thinking of the talk so long ago with Aloïs in her cedar closet. She still had the only thing she had ever owned, a JanSport D2 pack. Packing it and preparing to leave had become a constant project for her. Now was the day though, and all that thought excited her.

She rolled up her transcripts and stuffed them in her document folder, then combined it with her laptop. She already had clothing, food, and water. She had practiced with the pack's weight, planned where each item would be carried, and knew how to get things fast if she needed them. She could make a camp in the woods, carry it on a subway, and check it as luggage on a plane. She was ready for the world.

There was a knock at the apartment door.

Brighten Norbert was a stupid name, but he was one of the Bayside Norberts and worth a lot, which she couldn't care less about because technically she was worth two hundred times more. They had been having a tryst, and it seemed right when he had asked her to run away. *At least it did not seem wrong, which was fucking dandy*, she said to herself, laughing at her profanity.

Aloïs was retired, she saw him feeding birds in Central Park occasionally, looking quiet and grey, but she still loved him. She liked feeding birds with him when she could. But Norbert was someone who was impossible to love, and for that reason, he was a worthy companion. Norbert was full of himself. He couldn't care less what anyone thought.

Aloïs could scold Kelle with his eyes. Norbert could not punish her with his fists, and when he tried, she could put him into his place with a dark look under her black hair. Besides, he had no skill at punching despite being twice her weight. He had never done more than a little pancake could not hide.

And then there was her current guard, Winston Faulk. He was a tubulous rolling barrel of contempt for her. He spent most of his time telling war stories about his days in the SEALs to the Brazilian maids and making an insufferable ass of himself to the lesser security drones. Despite his self-image as an operator, he was actually a three-ring-binder type just like so many people in her father's company. Where Aloïs carried a single little pistol, Faulk carried a Desert Eagle, which he was forever drawing, field stripping, fondling, or otherwise making obierotic noises about its silver form or the size of the bullets it fired. If she had to hear, "Fucking big as pumpkins," again, she might just dose his coffee with something from her home reality physics lab.

No worries, she was leaving. Brighten had bribed two maids to sneak her out, and they couldn't give a shit where she went.

Maria, the first maid from Bahia, had a big laundry cart with a bottom shelf, which Kelle shoved her pack in and then crawled into herself. The second maid, also named Maria but from São Paulo, was currently performing fellatio on Faulk. Kelle was curious about this because she had promised to do the same with Brighten when she got away and wanted some tips from someone who was an expert, but there was no time. Brighten had sent her a picture of his own manhood standing erect, and she had used the metadata in the file to determine it was 11.43 centimeters in length. Purchasing a baby cucumber of the same size she was aghast to discover she was equipped with a gag reflex that made the operation Brighten desired almost impossible to achieve. Shit, even the idea of sticking it into her vagina seemed like a stretch. She wondered if she was equipped for sex at all. Tryst was an idea she understood—it meant holding hands and telling a complete doofus he was the greatest man in the world. Actually letting him skank around with her seemed too far to go.

Still, he had paid for her escape and made all the arrangements, and he did insist on something for repayment. So she had contemplated the cucumber and simply hoped it was over quickly.

The ride was uncomfortable. Kelle had dressed in vertical-striped corduroy flare pants that were chapping her thighs, a delicate slutty peasant's top, and a stage crew jacket from Wheatus that was not really warm enough under this cart. She had compromised on boots and worn her Dr. Martens, which was the only thing that was working in the setup.

She could tell Maria was taking her down the service elevator that security sometimes used to avoid the press. Then, it was out into the echoing garage where she stopped the cart and engaged in a quiet exchange. Kelle heard hushed nervous tones and an argument in Portuguese. Her tutors had never bothered with the language on the theory that only servants spoke it, anyway, although she had to learn fucking Slovenian so she could talk to a disgusting developer's shy girlfriend when they came over to schmooze the family over financing some boondoggle. Those were official dinners, and she would get a plastic-covered talking-point sheet from Dad's social secretary describing her duties, but that was less common now that they had hired the look-alike to stand in for her.

Why did men hire prostitutes? she wondered to herself.

Maria ducked under the sheet that covered her hiding place. "Get out, and into the truck."

She got out. There were two nervous men standing like sacks of winter wheat, flatfooted, slack-jawed, and with a slight squint that made Kelle think they were pressing down too hard on some really large butt plugs. One with a handlebar mustache said, "No fucking backpack."

Kelle said, "You, Angel Eyes, no fucking backpack, no princess of the fifty-fourth floor."

"Look here," the Angel Eyes "stand-in" tried to say, but the second one Kelle immediately thought of as Don Logan caught his arm. "No worries, Miss. Please step inside this truck. It is not comfortable, but we have to consider camouflage."

I bet you do, she thought, but she got into the truck and watched as the door slid closed. When it locked, she got out her panic button and triggered it.

The truck was filled with clothing, probably dirty stuff from the entire building. That was not so bad, nor was the bumpy ride. What was bad was that the truck's cab had a stereo system with its speakers installed by the back wall, and thus she was given a blast of idiotic Britney Spears balladeering. *Note to self,* she thought, *if ever assigned to break a terrorist's will, play Britney Spears.*

As for the panic button, she had to hide it. It was supposed to be kept near her body, and its signal would penetrate even from a big building. She cataloged places where she could conceal the little button, and there was nothing that would assure it stayed with her. She then nodded grimly. "Not how I thought this day would go."

She sat down and rubbed on the button to warm it up, and then gave it the "Rikers Island Snitch." She thought of the cucumber and blamed only herself for not getting some practice in the various natural means of concealment available to a free woman.

Grimly satisfied that the hiding place was successful, she opened her pack and pulled out some water. She knew she might have to leave her beloved pack behind, but before she did, she wanted to make sure the pack had yielded all of its goodies into her clothing.

Hydration was important, but it resulted in serious problems she had not contemplated. After drinking the bottle, she had to pee. She squatted in the corner of the truck and did so but lost the panic button. She had to find a handy wipe and put the panic button back.

After the water, she pulled a knife out of the pack. It was a little wood-handled CRAFTSMAN lock blade she used in the laboratory to open up shipping boxes. She kept it sharp enough to cut silk using a fine laboratory sharpener. It opened and closed as she tested it with no noise. The knife went in her waistband into a small slit she had sewn to carry in it.

Then she pulled out the Valium. Since her personal discussion on the efficacy of drug use, she had become someone who was rather prudish on the matter. However, given all the unique and rather unusual ways her body might be used tonight, the idea of powering through the thing a little high appealed to her. Instead of leaving it until the last minute, she took two of the pills and dry swallowed them then returned the bottle to the JanSport pack.

Kelle pulled out her engineer's notebook. She wrote a quick note to Aloïs and hid it in the corner of the truck. As benedictions go, she thought it was not bad. She had no doubt Aloïs would find this truck and would then find the book. Her note expressed her feelings for him but told him she was doing this of her own will.

She then pulled out a pack of business cards she had stolen from Winston Faulk. There were racks of suit coats that belonged to all of the powerful men in the building. The ones clean and in plastic which had been laundered but not unloaded each received one card.

The humor of the cards was esoteric. The phone number of the cards went to a vaguely racist and definitely sexist message where he promised to give any woman who called a trip to "o-town."

Her dad could not care about Kelle, but thirty powerful businessmen finding out his head of security was a "poon-hound" would make him care damn quick because their own daughters lived in the building with that round pervert.

The truck's rubber suspension hit a pothole, and she almost hit the ceiling. She yelled, "Should have chosen a better truck, assholes," but no one heard her. The sudden thrust had banged Kelle up, so she sat down and checked to see if she was bleeding, and damn if she had not cut her head on something. She pulled her little medical kit from the JanSport, a red plastic clamshell with a white medical cross, opened it up, and removed a gauze. From another pocket, she pulled her signal mirror. The truck was not well lit, so she had to also take out a hanging flashlight and affix it to rack filled with the plastic-covered suits. With this setup, she dressed her head wound, then figured out she had bled all over her shirt.

She worked diligently and quickly to clean her wound, then returned all the of minutia of her sudden traumatic care event back into the pack right where they belonged. The ride was taking longer than she expected, so she arranged the pack for support, pulled her earbuds into her ears, and dialed on a song from her collection.

After ten more minutes, the truck stopped and the door opened, and she immediately realized that things were not going to turn out how she had planned. Besides the two idiots that had picked her up that she had dubbed "Angel Eyes" and "Don Logan," there were now three more men in stupid black fatigues and face masks. Brighten stood nervously behind the five men, scared out of his wits.

"Brighten, you ignorant fucking Lorax, what the fuck have you done?" Kelle yelled.

Two of the new men in masks climbed into the truck and manhandled her roughly out. One of the men, as he was pulling and yanking on her, took numerous chances to cop a feel. It seriously pissed her off, and she promised to find out who the man was and have his balls cut off with a sharp knife. As they threw her roughly to the floor, Brighten yelled, "I had no choice, Kelle."

"You had no choice," she replied. "Well, just keep saying that to yourself. Do you think Angel Eyes and Don Logan are going to thank you when one of these masked men maximally demote them to pushing up daisies with their foreheads?"

The masked man who had not touched her yet said, "Shut up." Only it was not a masked man in turned out. It was a masked woman.

The two masked men then grabbed her again and pulled her to her feet. She tried to struggle, but their grips tightened. *God,* she thought, *fucking Valium rocks,* as the drug she took kicked in. She would be scared shitless without the stuff. Her earbuds slipped out as she struggled, but she did not care. Despite the pain of their grips, she was able to land a very satisfying kick to one man's groin. He went to the ground screaming, and the other masked man slapped her, but in doing so, he lost his grip.

She stomped his foot, not an effective strategy given her weight, but it allowed her a chance to run. It was a warehouse filled with crates on orange shelves, and in the center was a bed with lights set up around it and a set of chains at the far corner. She came up short as she saw that and yelled, "Fuck that," then ducked as Angel Eyes tried to take her down. He ended up on the bed face down, so she rewarded him with a very satisfying groin kick, her boots really grinding the man's jewels into his body. But the fun was cut short as Don Logan and one of the masked men made a grab at her.

She turned and stepped away as they collided with each other and then were further entangled with Angel Eyes, tears streaming from his face, getting up from the bed.

She was going to make a break for the other direction when the woman in the mask clotheslined her. "Will you idiots get her under control?"

The four men tackled her and each took an arm or leg as she spit and bit at them, screaming in rage. She was too small though, and they were able to throw her onto the bed.

It was then a few minutes while she made getting shackles on her legs and arms expensive. They tried to keep hold of her limbs and guide them into the clasps, but she was able to keep pulling one leg or arm away, where upon she would cause damage to the person on that side. She got a thumb into a nose, a kick to the neck, and bit one of the men on the cheek.

Finally, the woman in the mask said, "For heaven's sake, she is ninety pounds." She pulled a knife, waded in, and cut away Kelle's shoes as she struggled, then yelled, "You let them lock you or I will scar your face!"

Brighten stood behind them "Brighten, you are a great, big, giant cock!" she yelled.

Brighten says, "Honey, I had to."

The clasps went on, and then Kelle was helpless. Screaming louder she yelled, "You massive imbecile Brighten, you have killed me. Do you think these idiots want to teach me calculus?"

The four men backed away, and the woman in the mask turned and pulled it off. She had green hair and very light, almost ghostly, skin. She looked at Kelle and said, "Now set the damn camera up." She turned and walked to another car, a Subaru Sport in gaudy yellow.

The men started setting up the camera as Brighten walked up to the bed. "It is a scam baby," he said. He was dressed in the same stupid black fatigues the rest were, but for some damn reason, he had wrapped his neck with an ascot. "I could not get money from my dad for us to run away. I only had a half million in the bank; we need ten to go to Brazil!"

"Brazil, you fucking idiot," she yelled. "Why Brazil? No one would have cared where we were. My dad's security would have just watched us. You sad dick-flute!" Kelle was so angry she could spit.

Then there is an inexplicably loud sound, a gun-shot. Kelle tried to sit up and saw that Brighten's eyes were bulging. The green-haired woman had fired a nine-millimeter pistol into the side of his head. She looked at his face as he lost all human thought, and she closed her eyes, imagining what had happened to the fool.

The round, traveling at just short of three-hundred meters per second, penetrated through the left parietal bone, losing twenty-five or so meters per second of speed in the process. Still moving at more than the speed of sound, the bullet then destroyed a mass of white brain matter, causing immediate anopia in part of the Brighten's visual spectrum, while a surging wave of liquid caused massive damage throughout the lobe, resulting in immediate deafness and a loss of semantic memory building. The bullet then began to tumble in the dense, but liquid matter, causing it to take a veering path, cutting into the parietal lobe causing not only agnosia but also anosognosia. It finished coming to rest between the victim's eyes, lodged in the grey matter of the frontal lobe.

In the slow roll of time, Kelle opened her eyes and fixed them on Brighten, noting with her scientific self what was happening. The headshot triggered an immediate response, though the opposite of what might be anticipated. Brighten's head jerked toward the gun, at least until the first spray of blood leaving the wound caused it to return to its original position. The path of the bullet essentially blinded and deafened Brighten in a fraction of a second, but his mind remained functioning. As Kelle watched in slow motion, she saw euphoria sketch across Brighten's face. The severe brain damage removed the part of his thought processes that could process dread, creating what showed on his face, a sense of euphoria, like the world had become simpler and more clear.

He swayed slightly as muscle memory kept Brighten standing for the first second or two. He lifted his hands a little and locked his bulged eyes on her with recognition, like that a child would have for a parent. This lasted for only a second, and then he lost his smile and his face sagged. This was merely a reflexive response caused by the various circuits continuing to do what they intended to do before the brain had suffered the traumatic injury.

In the seconds Brighten remained standing, Kelle noted his mouth twitches that came with trauma to Broca's area and the rigidity of the neck muscles that showed a general shutdown of the brain. No matter how bad all this was and how crippled he might have become, Kelle saw a spurt of blood from the initial wound that splashed the woman in the face.

It was the blood loss Kelle knew which would kill poor Brighten. She watched the blood spurt out and knew that inside of Brighten's body things were breaking down. His heart was beating about one hundred times per minute. The blood volume being lost from the wound is about 50 milliliters per beat. For the three seconds that he remained standing upright after the bullet had finished its wrecking travel through the man's head, he lost nearly half of a liter of blood.

He then collapsed like a poleaxed deer. He started to shake as his heart beat faster, and the blood came out faster with each beat. After twenty-three seconds, he went into Cheyne-Stokes breathing and then cardiac arrest. He died in the next minute, never to return to the Earth.

Kelle looked up from the body at the woman. "Why did you do that?" She controlled her rage as best she could, terrible anger replacing fear.

The woman laughed and turned away.

"Answer me," Kelle said quietly.

Angel Eyes, wounded and seething, was setting up the video camera. Hearing her, he said, "Shut up."

Kelle looked back down and stared at the dead man on the floor. The Valium is not enough. What did Aloïs tell her? Be a little girl. Make them empathize. She started to tear up and said, "You will kill me, right?"

The two remaining masked kidnappers removed their masks. One was a younger man with frizzy blond hair. He replied to her, "You forget that. Be pleasant, and we will get you home."

"He was my boyfriend," she said. Fucking Brighten the Lorax who was nothing more now than a sad, twitching bundle on the floor. The difference between her and him was that she was worth hundreds of times more money, but unlike her, his parents would have paid the ransom. They obviously did not know that.

"Sorry," the thug said. He brushed his thin hair, then pulled a shotgun microphone from his pocket. It was broken. He looked at her with daggers in his eyes and yelled to their leader, the woman with green hair, "Bitch broke the microphone!"

The woman walked up and looked at it. "The camera has a microphone, no?"

He looked at the camera standing on a tripod aimed at Kelle, "Not a good one. This was a Sanken. Great sound."

"Are you kidding me? Who cares?" she replied, then stalked away.

The kid looked back at Kelle, "This thing costs five hundred, and you broke it."

Kelle teared up, though it was hard to do. "I am ever so sorry; she should not have treated you that way."

The kid said, "Yeah." Then he turned to fiddle with the camera.

Kelle seethed great gobbets of hate at her captors, her mind drawing every sort of brutal ending for them that could be imagined a person her age might know. Brighten was an idiot. She knew he was an idiot. Idiots do not deserve death sentences. She thought of how close corporate security was by now. They knew she was gone, and they had her tracker, designed to be picked up by cell towers all the way through the city and probably even in the country. Aloïs had told her that rescues now were four and in. No hostage situations with tense rows of trigger-happy cops would be permitted. Her father hated that Patty Hearst shit. When four security agents had arrived at the scene and were ready, they charged the bad guys who, just like these simple fucks, would probably still be standing around arguing about what to do next.

What was she thinking? Faulk was getting his knob polished, and there was no guarantee any of the three-ring-binder people had noticed her alarm had been tripped when she was thrown around. If Maria reported her missing, it would be around midnight, and how forthcoming would she be? Of course, it was even possible that her double had moved into her room, and the company had washed its hands of her.

They had their little movie ready, so the woman, blood still drenching her black cardigan, threw a newspaper on Kelle's belly and said, "Start the camera."

The blond kid turned on the camera, and Angel Eyes read from a paper. "We of the Nationalist White Klan have taken your daughter and demand 450 million dollars in five-dollar bills delivered to the place we designate in the next twenty-two hours, or our next video will be much more graphic and sent to InfoWars, who have agreed to show it to every red-blooded American tired of being shoved around by communist simps. This is your only warning."

The blond kid turned off the camera. Kelle, still in shackles, said, "Twenty thousand pounds."

The one she called Logan stopped and said, "What the hell are you on about?"

Kelle replied, "Ten tons, genius. You are idiots. You just asked for ten tons of cash."

The blond kid and Angel Eyes came up and said, "Why do you say that?"

"Each bill weighs a gram. You just asked for nine million of them. Nine metric tons plus the bags or boxes they are crated in. Does that stupid SUV there even hold that much, or do you have an army truck somewhere?" Kelle said.

The older of the formerly masked men came up and said, "Beejie, is she right about how much money that is?"

The green-haired woman laughed. "They won't pay that much for her. One of our allies will step in, talk reason into us, and we will get our real pay when we get to St. Petersburg." She paused and then said, "Get this place ready, we will be leaving tomorrow for the safe house."

They all walked away, leaving the green-haired woman to fiddle around with a blocky satellite phone. She rewound the tape in the camera, messed with the camera's controls, and then ran a cable from the phone to the camera's side.

"What is your real plan?" Kelle asked the woman.

The woman set the camera running and looked over at her. "Not a cinema drama, *cher fils*. I am not the bad guy who runs her mouth to the heroine so she can foil the plan with her skills."

Kelle laid back on the bed. "I am just saying. The first two you let their faces be seen. The second two let me see their faces. And I have seen your face. Obviously, I am dead, so you cannot tell me what is happening?"

The woman left the camera and walked up to Kelle chained down on the bed. "No, darling, still not a movie."

"Ok, but I told the blond guy he was cute, and Angel Eyes you would kill him. You think I am a cute seventeen-year-old, but I have three Ph. Ds in subjects you cannot even pronounce, and my father is the third richest man in the world, so it's rich you killed my boyfriend, whose father actually loves him and would pay a lot to get him back.

The woman laughed, "Oh, your daddy loves you. He would move worlds to save you. He would give away all of his secrets. You are such an entitled princess you do not realize that. There is more than money, and he will pay it to me." She unplugged the phone, turned, and left Kelle, shutting off the lights as she went.

With the lights off, the huge warehouse became a closet of darkness. Kelle wished she had her backpack, but that was beyond any hope. Instead, she started to slowly work her wrists in the shackles. In all of the struggles and pain, she had made sure that the idiots did not double lock the shackles and did not check to see that her hands were barely bigger than her wrists.

She grimaced and scraped her right wrist until it was bleeding a little, then used the lubricant to slowly twist and pull her hand through. With that hand free, she grabbed for her waistband and clawed out her knife, opening it with her mouth and pulling the corkscrew out. She then reached over to her left hand to release it, but the blood that allowed her out of the clasps caused the blade to spin off into the darkness.

"Fuck," she said.

"Do not curse," came a voice from the darkness. It was Aloïs.

Kelle started to say something, but he put his hand on her mouth. In her ear, he asked, "How many?"

"Five," she whispered back. "How many of you?"

"Just me." His voice was pitched low. "Faulk is dead, and your dad is having a fit."

"Dad would not allow a rescue," she stated.

Aloïs was quiet. Kelle then heard him start undressing. In the wan light, she noticed he was wearing a Kevlar jumpsuit under his battle dress. It fit him like a glove. He peeled it off himself, leaving him in spandex shorts and a top. He draped the Kevlar on her and started working on the shackles.

"No, Aloïs. Put your armor back on."

"Shut up," he said. He had never said something to her in that tone before.

She clenched her fist and pulled away from his work on her shackles. "Don't tell me to shut up."

"You see, Kelle, this is the problem. You have a brain the size of a planet, but no one has equipped you for the iconic American pop culture comeback. Not really. I thought for twenty years my name was Shut Up. Now let me get you out of these shackles."

Kelle relented. "Clever," she said.

"Not me, Joe Namath." He released all four shackles, then pushed her down on the bed, grabbed her legs, and started to pull the Kevlar body suit onto her. "When we make a break for it, grab my belt buckle and keep on me. I have a distraction planned in a few moments."

"Aloïs, how did you learn to interrogate people?" she asked.

He looked at her and roughed her hair. "I took some advice from Errol Morris. Shut up and listen."

The crackling sound of speakers came to life out on the warehouse floor with the static of an expectant announcement. Aloïs finished strapping Kelle into the armor. "Grab my belt now," he said. She did.

The warehouse's audio system started playing the chorus of "Walk Away Renée." It was deafening, like someone had turned a stereo receiver up to eleven. Aloïs broke a chem light, but it only provided a little light, like it was broken and did not work. It was enough to show that he had a little German lemon-squeezer automatic in his hand. He lowered night vision goggles in front of his eyes and waived the chem light around, then threw it into the darkness.

The music screamed as they ran into the darkness of the cavern-like space of the warehouse. Kelle could only see glimpses of the orange warehouse trestle shelves and an occasional mound of packaged goods. Then they turned a corner, and Kelle could hear Aloïs's gun spit quietly three times, like the sound of an old-fashioned phone book being slapped on the wall. One of the bad guys was down, the blond kid. He had a hole in his head and two in his chest and had a look of surprise on his face.

They heard screaming in the distance, and Aloïs stopped. The screaming went on, and he said, "One of the bear traps."

Kelle asked, "How long have you been in this warehouse?"

"Long enough to drop a few bear traps," Aloïs replied, his face a familiar outline in the darkness.

They alternately ran and crept along the warehouse racks. Then he stopped them, hesitated, and stepped out from the cover of a crate stack, fired three times. Snap, snap, snap! Then returned to cover.

A tornado of bullets was the response, the rounds pinging around them and shredding crates. Aloïs grunted and pulled her undercover. He was bleeding from his abdomen. *"Sohn einer Hündin!"* he said in some foreign tongue.

"Aloïs!"

He dropped a magazine from his pistol and replaced it. *"Arschgeige!"* he yelled, as if to the shooters. "Damn. We are about ten meters from the door. Get ready to run."

"Right behind you."

"Nope, I need to convince Flachwichser and his buddy Fickfehler to give up this shit."

More bullets struck around them. She said in the noise, close to his ear. "No."

"Look, young Miss." He grunted in pain. "Seventy-four I am, nothing left but pigeons in the park."

Kelle had started crying. "Don't you fucking say that."

"Dr. Brainerd," he said and touched her cheek with his bloody hand. She grabbed his hand and kissed it, but he pulled it away.

It was the first time anyone had called her that. She had a doctorate just this year, but who calls a seventeen-year-old "Doctor" unless they are Doogie Hauser?

"I love you, Aloïs," she said with all of her heart.

"Shut up." His eyes were a fury of concentration.

Kelle was speechless as another barrage of bullets splashed around them and the song started over at the beginning. "Pleasant soundtrack, Cameron Crowe."

Aloïs said, "There you go. Quote something stupid when you are scared. It is better than some sappy dialogue that only makes creative writing professors happy." He coughed hard then said, "Doesn't even have to make sense. Everyone will assume you are smarter than they are."

Aloïs got to his knees. "You need to find my *Korpsbruder*, Regulus, and tell him this." He stopped and then said, *"Du hattest recht, ich bin gestorben und habe ein Mädchen beschützt."*

"What does it mean? Where is this Regulus?" she asked, flinching from the splinters of machine gun fire.

"Never mind what it means. And Regulus is not where, he is when. 2017 in Ybor City. Look for a sculpture show with a bunch of absurd yellow junk. He will be the smug bastard next to the stuff."

"You can do that yourself," she said.

"Sure, but let's call it insurance. Run now!" he yelled.

Eleven days later, Kelle saw the view from the kidnapper's camera, which had been accidentally switched on a minute before. She digitized the footage and then played it back on her computer. In it, she could see herself break from cover as someone threw a flashing strobe light into the open, dressed in a huge Kevlar bodysuit. Bullets caused sparks around her, but the fire changed direction as Aloïs burst from cover. The music was haunting, telling Renee to walk away, so she cut the sound and set the video to slow motion. Aloïs had a wild smile on his face, his long, gray and black hair floating in the air, his hands holding the pistol in front of his face as he advanced on the men firing Kalashnikov rifles in return. *"Hakkaa päälle!"* she remembered he had yelled as he advanced. She saw he was hit and hit again, and then another time, but he kept running forward screaming in a tongue she had never heard him use before; she had thought he was German. *"Jumala nähdä minut! Tuo minun teräs!"* Both men were hit, but Aloïs fell as well. The camera toppled as her first love collapsed into it, and she saw one of the gunmen had taken aim at her own back. Then, the heaped form of Aloïs rolled with great effort and started firing rapidly into the man with a rifle he grabbed from the floor. The captor with the rifle turned and fired at Aloïs and the camera, and when the exchange was over, nothing moved but the falling of small bits of cloth, dancing in the strobing flash of firelights.

SHAKING MAN

DATE: JANUARY 12, 2018
LOCATION: PETERBOROUGH, NEW HAMPSHIRE

I stared blankly at the picture of Rains-a-Lot I had found in the archives of Dustin-Rhodes Company. In my hand, I played with two big pink pills. I knew I was having light seizures again—that feeling of flying over the world of Virdea, dumb but free, with amazing hearing and the eyesight of the gods. Then finding myself in my seizure nest where I had retreated: back hurting, tongue bitten, dehydrated, and confused.

So far, I was coming back from the seizures, but basically being a cowardly person, I was scared every night that some piece of me was breaking off, never to return. There was no one I could ever talk to about this. I could only keep my eye on my goal. I switched on the music on my computer, which for some reason chose a Lady Gaga album to play.

The pills were still in my hand. I swallowed them and chased them with a Caffeine-free Diet Coke. The picture of Rains-a-Lot was in the middle of a crazy spiral of documents that defined an amazing life, and one of the best pieces of historical detective work I had ever put together. I was not even sure if I cared that it was all madness. Fuck it. I made sure my phone was set to "up yours," then went into the work room.

You see, Dustin-Rhodes lost a purple 1957 Chevy in Bashful, Kansas in August 1960, the same day a thermal inversion destroyed the town. Bashful was remembered, to this day, by a fanatic group of local Kansas historians who celebrated the myths and memories of the community, especially the paranormal aspects of the town's demise and its connections to the land of Virdea.

All was well and good.

Dustin-Rhodes had stopped operations in the late 1980s and abandoned its tax and employee records in a building in Des Moines, Iowa, where I found out that the 1957 Chevy was issued to Ivy d'Seille and Rains-a-Lot. The d'Seille file was fairly mundane, but the Rains-a-Lot file had an odd quirk: it used a Bureau of Indian Affairs (BIA) tax number to identify Rains-a-Lot instead of a Social Security number. This was not unheard of in the 1930s and 1940s when Social Security cards were less common, but by 1960 nearly all American Indians had, in some form, abandoned the old BIA identifications, which was originally created to track ration issuing during the Civil War. One advantage of that number, though, was that the obsolete records were easy to claim through the Freedom of Information Act (FOIA), and those records confirmed my growing realization that this was far from a normal investigation.

I opened the brown envelope that contained my FOIA request documents, discarding the receipt for photocopy payments, and eagerly pulled out the first piece of paper. It was a beautiful photocopy of a ration document dated 1866 from the Fifth Infantry Regiment. The purpose of the document was to account for the disbursement of rations to a band of Lakota, listing the individual members of the band receiving meals of hard tack, salted pork, desiccated vegetable cubes, and cans of "sweet milk." In a neat hand, some infantry sergeant had recorded first a BIA identification number, then a name, then an estimated age, for each person receiving the ration.

I marveled at the name halfway down the list. Rains-Often-Child, son of Laughing Bear, BIA# 66-1120, age four. I imagined the poor sergeant, assaulted by lines of unusual names, often poorly translated by civilian employees who did not know the language they claimed expertise in, at least not well enough to follow small nuances, trying to list each identity in English. For the sergeant, names were fixed things placing him into time, space, and ancestry. For the Lakota, at least until they won fame, names described events of pride, inside jokes, or spiritual concepts, and they could change over time as the person who own it evolved. A Lakota could tell someone the names they had held, and in that way, it would tell their own life story. Sergeant McGann, who was trying to fix down the person in front of him drawing rations, wanted that name to be frozen in time. BIA numbers did just that. It tried to take the Child-born-in-the-Rain, who as a teenage warrior would be called the Rains-a-Lot and then be named Jim Smith, and turn him into the easy to record, track, control, and dismiss 66-1120.

The second document in the bundle showed this. It was a certificate of adoption with the names of both parents blank for One (1) Child, Indian, 14-15 years of age, Orphan, Number 66-1120. Dated 1877 and witnessed by two Quaker missionaries. It declares that the child "Unnamed" would become the child, as if by natural birth, of Marlow Smith and his wife Blue Flower.

In the place where the adopting parents were to sign, a mysterious signature appeared, "Lt. Col. McGriffin Bailey, 3rd U.S. Cavalry," as if there was no need to have Marlow or his wife acknowledge the adoption. I pinned the paper onto my wall and added the rationing document above it, then stuck the more modern picture of Rains-a-Lot between them.

The next document was a BIA form for entry into the Quaker School at Fresh Wells in 1878. Gone was Rains-a-Lot, the Lakota. Now there appeared Jim Smith; a Cherokee of "mixed breed." It was an interesting switch in the young man's life. The earlier Rains-a-Lot was full-blooded Lakota, although of what particular band no one had ever recorded. In the thinking of racialists in that era, even if Rains-a-Lot had been born of a Lakota parent and a Cherokee parent, he would still be an Indian. A single white parent and a single Indian parent were all that could result in the designation of "mixed breed." Somehow, through mistake or subterfuge, Rains-a-Lot had added notional white ancestry to his makeup.

Rains-a-Lot must have been a good student. The Quaker School at Fresh Wells was not so much a grammar school as a school where the Quakers, a fairly open-minded sect, taught American Indians how to live in white society. The students would learn how to tend a forty-acre farm, how to do sums and keep farm accounts, how to dress in proper Sunday attire, and how to say and spell out 180 essential words in English, and they were discouraged from drinking, sex, and smoking by watching scientific demonstrations where a baby pig was killed with a pint of bourbon. Despite the limitations of this school, the next document was a letter from the headmaster.

July 2nd, 1882

To whom it may concern,

This letter is in support of my best pupil, Jim Smith. When Master Smith first arrived at my class he was an ill-dressed, silent, angry savage who had never learned even the most rudimentary skills to feed, bathe, or clothe himself. In just three years, he has blossomed to an amazing member of our community and is a credit to the white part of his blood and to God. He has learned to read rapidly, knows each of the presidents by heart in the order of their service, has acquired his letters and sums, and has actually started on the difficult road of mastering Greek, French, and Latin.

It is my belief that Master Smith has been completely civilized in his short years with us, learning to turn the other cheek, smile at adversity and walk with his head held high as a man of peace. For this reason, I have drafted this letter to your university for consideration with the hopes that you will see fit to include Master Smith in your class for 1882.

Thank you for your consideration.
Bailey Mission,
Headmaster,
Fresh Wells School

The final document was simply a photocopy of a file card listing the activation of BIA Number 66-1120 in 1943 with the name change of Rains-a-Lot, 82 years old, with the Social Security Administration in the community of Prairie City, Iowa.

The music coming out of my computer was upbeat, so I sang along with Lady Gaga's "Born This Way" while looking at the picture of Rains-a-Lot at, what was chronologically, 92 years old when it was taken in 1953.

The picture was of a man in his late thirties.

I pinned the copy of the 1943 BIA card to the wall with a flourish, doing a small dance step to the time of the music. *So many oddities,* I thought. A photocopy of the Drake Times-Delphic, volume 3, number 3 of December 1886 with an article on page 15 by a J. R. Smith discussing the rights of the Plains Indians. An article by Jimmy Smith of Drake University in the October 1887 edition of *Challenge Magazine* recounting the Battle of the Four Lakes as the true ending of the ability of "Native Americans" to fight their way to any reasonable outcome. And, most haunting, on page 149 of the 1902 Drake University yearbook *The Quax*, oddly enough published in 1901, a poem from Law School alumni Jimmy J.R. Smith called the "Boy that Ate Custer's Heart."

The song changes to "Million Reasons" as I dance about in front of the board, pinning the photocopies one at a time to the wall.

"The Boy That Ate Custer's Heart"—that says so much. I break into a Lady Gaga inspired "sandwich slap" while the court documents come out. "J" Smith files for relief from the BIA on behalf of the Lakota, and the ultimate irony, is denied standing as a "white attorney not under contract by any Lakota tribe." An old photograph of soldiers posing in front of dead bodies at Wounded Knee and intensely angry Rains-a-Lot standing behind them. An account of an officer found scalped several days later with a report of the freak tornado that hit near Pine Ridge. It was through that freak tornado and act of violence that Rains-a-Lot apparently traveled to Virdea, and at some point, returned to the modern era of Earth intact.

My walking stick Grandfather popped into my hands. Such a strange icon to carry, a stick whose cracked wood formed the face of an old man. I danced with Grandfather as I regarded the information on my walls. Grandfather was always up for some fun and would often come up with better ideas on stubborn problems than I could.

The Lady Gaga songs were running down, and I was out of breath. Plus, if I sang any more of the lyrics to myself, I would exceed fair use restrictions and have to start paying royalties. It was then that I noticed my vision dimming at the edges, and I could feel the mass of my forebrain start to twist about. One of my earliest experiences of epilepsy, before I knew I had seizures, was a terrible four-part experience that I, like many people with my medical condition, call an aura. It starts with a fading of the peripheral vision.

If you discount a single experience with a communist professor in Mexico, and one time when I had to take a small dose of narcotics to get out of a court-ordered rehabilitation scheme, I had largely lived my life drug-free. Well, I used to drink cough syrup in high school—but you try to deal with that place sober. Largely lacking addictive traits, and with a mind that was in some ways always in an altered state, drugs were not appealing.

The thing with my brain had been called idiopathic epilepsy. Idiopathic just means the poor doctors feel like idiots because they have no idea why I have bouts of falling over and becoming a human martini mixer. After the edges of my vision go, the feeling I have a twisted knot in my head starts to get bigger. By now, I have pulled over my car, abandoned my grocery cart in the hands of a startled teenage stock clerk, and begun looking for a safe place to hide. By luck, this one was in my house.

People are idiots. Paramedics are well-meaning. The combination of the two is deadly. People think they know how to treat epilepsy because they have watched it on Marcus Welby, M.D. They stick things in my mouth (which breaks my teeth), hold my tongue to keep me from swallowing it (depriving me of air and causing me to bite both it and them), or they try to restrain my flailing. At times, they have checked to see if I am faking by cutting me with a pocketknife, putting a cigarette out on my skin, pulling out clumps of hair, and hyperextending my fingers.

Paramedics know each minute I suffer from seizures is a minute I might have permanent brain damage. So they will ask for and get permission to inject me with one of a range of drugs that they may (or may not) have in their medical kits. Of all of them, Valium has been the only one that works without allergic reactions. If they know about the allergic reactions and are ready, they can then treat me. At least until I get to the hospital, where I have to hope the medical team in admitting both recognizes the severity of my case, reads the multitude of medical alert devices hanging from my body like Shadowrun fetishes, and watch me like a hawk when I start to do any one of a number of crazy things.

By the time the second part of my aura is cranking along, I have done my ritual. I pee. I drink as much water as I can. I may be out for days, and dehydration has been a problem in the past. I swallow some more Valproate because what the hell, maybe it will work. I write on my chest in Sharpie EPILEPSY_NOT_DRUGS. At happier times in my life, I would also write TESLA_WAS_ROBBED. At sadder times in my life, I wrote DO_NOT_REVIVE. Once I wrote PLACE_FRONT_TO_ENEMY. Not sure where I got the last one.

I take off restrictive clothes. I hide documents in my seizure backpack, which has photocopies of the ones I will need. I make myself a nest. Then, I wait.

Then I rapidly experience what I think of as a brain dump. Dead people will talk to me. I will go back to the field with at the burning plane in it. I will see again all the horrible things I do not want to see. Gradually, though, this is replaced with the feeling of soaring over a green land filled with amazing things. My eyesight will grow sharp. I hear wonderful sounds. My sense of taste falls away, as does my sense of smell. I feel the warmth of pin feathers and sense the amazing ability to move naturally through another dimension by bending my wings.

I never have any memory of the next horseman of epilepsy, the actual seizure. I do remember the dreaming.

FIGHT AT LARK FIELD

DATE: 4TH DAY OF THE BEAR, 3684
LOCATION: LARK FIELD, GREAT MEADOWS, VIRDEA

Writers have a problem. When they create a story, they need to create a consistent narrative point of view that allows the reader a place to enter it. Early in the secret world of writer's school, they learn which person they should be at what time. Or they do not, and they will never write anything of any worth. Writers say that they are exploring the concept of person and give each person a number to tell them apart.

First-person is a common point of view.

I pick up a sword. I swing the sword.

It is a cozy way to write but has three limitations. The first is that eventually, your word processor runs out of the letter "I." This letter in English is really a tricky bastard because it looks so much like an "L," or sometimes a "J," that you get buggered quickly when you have paragraphs littered with it.

The second problem with first-person is to deal with the issue of omnipotence. The author of this book is Nelson McKeeby, the forty-eight-year-old autistic man who we last left preparing for an epileptic seizure. His life revolves around his disability, which happens to be killing him; his past, which he sometimes remembers fitfully; and whatever story he is telling at that second. His literary agent likes to point out he has a rather-wandering way of telling stories, "Like a caffeinated monkey got a hold of a hash pipe." He also is not omnipotent. If he had been, he would have, instead of trying to lock down the life story of an American Indian time traveler, been observing in first-person the sexual escapades of the five people living in the apartment next to him, which would have made him a best-selling author when he published it under the title *The Fifty-First Shade*.

What do you do when your narrator is not there to tell the audience what they are seeing? Take this instance at the edge of Lark Field by the murmuring waters of the Bristlebrook. Blocking the path northward across the Yellow King Road, which at this point of its thousand-mile journey is a cowpath climbing into the Great Meadows, is an 'army.' The careful reader will note the use of punctuations around the word. If an army consists of hundreds of men and women, mostly trained as farmers and holding farm instruments, stiffened by a single regiment of the Meadow Rangers, then you have one right here. If instead, when you think of an army, you think of 568 men armored in cocoons of steel and armed with forged swords capable of hacking a human arm from its accustomed moorings, then perhaps you are thinking of the military unit that is marching out into the middle of the field to face the farmers.

Now, the author has some choices here to help the reader out.

Creative writing classes across the planet have warned against the second person, which is talking in the "you" form to the reader.

Right about the time you first read this chapter, in Covington, Oregon, a gentleman named Bayle Prestley is desperately searching for rolling papers to wrap up his newly grown organic marijuana. His sister, for his recent birthday, has given him a copy of this book, which she bought at a used bookstore. Desperate, he rips a page out of the first edition copy that was signed by Nelson McKeeby, rolls himself a fatty, and smokes up. Bayle, who will read this same book 164 days later, will not realize what he has done until he reads the next sentence. Bayle, you just lost a pile of cash by destroying a first edition that your sister had asked me to sign directly to you. Plus, your weed is trash, and the ink in the papers that make this book cause impotence when you smoke them. Not really, but it made you wonder, did it not?

Second person is a bit brain twisty if you think, "What if he had read that same paragraph the day before he ripped the page out?" you could ask. But when I discuss you and claim you are doing something, you can always do it differently. So second person is this swirl of weirdness that authors work hard to avoid. I should probably avoid it, but that would require a rewrite and you are already reading this book, so that is impossible.

Which brings us to third person, the king of narratives.

If you were to sit up in a tree and watch the approaching armies, noting the precision of the gleaming metal columns, the palpable fear of the green-dressed farmers holding glaives that were hammered from useful bits of metals in a farrier's forge and are not even properly heat treated, you would be in the realm of distant third. There is not a whole lot of emotion here, just an establishing shot of actions and acts. A mass of ravens and crows have gathered in the trees. The wind is blowing the green grass of the field. Trees creak under their foliage, some of which still has the spectacular colors of fall.

The main issue with distant third is that it fails at getting the reader inside the characters' heads. For that, we use close third. We place our camera just past the shoulder of one of the subjects, tie it off there, and wire its sensorium into the mind of the person being followed. For example, let's enter Jarweed, a scout for the Second Host of the Yellow King's Vasting.

Jarweed had circled the farmers. The *fucking amateurs,* or so he thought of them, were in array out in the damn field, and it was not a trap. They had no fucking reserves. He noted how now was the time to act. Gaining confidence, he spurred his horse around and tore out into the field, riding hard to impress his commanders. He would rush down the line of hicks, taunting them with the fact their wives would be moaning under him before nightfall. As he started his run, he felt an incredible pain in his shoulder, and then another in his neck. He tried to reign up and feel what had happened, but he fell dead from two arrows shot by Hamilvar, the champion archer of the Meadowland Rangers.

Well, shit. You see some issues with close third. First, Jarweed is not a perfect narrator. His duty was to scout for the Yellow King. He was too profane and self-absorbed to do that right. He inaccurately assessed the tactical danger he faced even as he accurately noted the peasants lacked reserves, and then to make things worse, he gets killed before he is done giving us a good narrative. Change close third viewpoints too often, and the audience gets confused like they are trying to understand an episode of *Lost* in its last season.

Two other issues. Close third is supposed to let the reader gain some empathy for the character being followed, and Jarweed was a little prick at best, hard to gain empathy for a murderous rodent like him, though we all shine under God's light. Plus, his language has totally fucked up any chance McKeeby had of pawning this book off to the YA (Young Adult) trade. Now, Nelson might as well throw in some gratuitous sex at some point as reader service to make sure everyone knows this is a real epic romp.

The final issue with close third is that while we were paying attention to Jarweed, other things were happening in the field. And since we lost that overarching point of view, we will have to look around to find it.

Could it be Severn's daily erection? Severn is a sixteen-year-old boy holding one of those poorly made glaives next to Landy, the woman he has loved since he was eight. She has recently told him she would give herself to him if they lived through the battle, and that was exciting, until he saw the soldiers of the Yellow King march onto the field of battle. At that point, he had screamed to the gods of how unfair life was. Then the hero, Hamilvar, shot the horseman as he taunted the doomed peasants, and Severn felt the frisson in Landy's hand as she touched his elbow, causing the sudden arrival of an ironic and mistimed boner.

It is not that, though.

Could it be that the raven, Thndry, sitting in a brush Sycamore looking distastefully at the battlefield has begun to question the sanity of humans? Ravens only eat human meat when they are starving because it does not "finish well," the raven term for the quality of defecation. Crows love human meat. Ravens consider crows as stupid simian relatives whose occupation was mostly to eat and shit. There was some envy though because crows could eat all sorts of things that ravens would find hard to finish well, but there was also a degree of snobbish superiority. Thndry danced a small step and emoted to his flock mate, Rndrl. "Hopeful crows."

The crows were yelling, "Meat, meat."

Rndrl scratched with his beak and replied, "Microcephalic idiots."

Thndry had the curiosity of all ravens and thus would stay and watch the horrible contest below, but he was not happy about it. The forest peasants of the Great Meadows were kind to ravens, setting out gifts of food and preserving their nests. There was talk about how they could help the poor people, but it was just talk. It was beyond memory since a conspiracy of ravens had formed.

As interesting as close third is for following ravens, they also were missing many clues. It sometimes falls upon an omnipotent narrator, equipped with a tool kit that allows him/her to move nimbly about in time and space, and thus point out the obvious. And the obvious is that at this very second in Virdea (as elusive as the concept of linear time is in this land) and at this very place (in a land where maps are rare and cherished as the greatest art of humankind), two amazing events are/were occurring that are/were presaged by two seemingly mundane happenings. The first happening was a slight increase in wind velocity and the beginning of a notable circular pattern in its motion. The second was that Thndry, the most respected of ravens, squawked and fell from the tree.

Disturbed by both events, the rest of the ravens went to investigate Thndry. They found him on the ground shaking. It was what they called "God Mount." For a decade, a dark intelligence had occasionally taken over the mind of one of the ravens, and amazing things would result. It had chosen Thndry this time, whose mind was expanding in an attempt to encompass the being with an intellect five to nine times the size of the physical capacity of the organic thinking unit the raven possessed.

And what only an omnipotent narrator could know was that in 2018 the author Nelson McKeeby was having a seizure because his own mind could not fit entirely within a raven's brain. It was true irony that Nelson would only discover in conversation with a disembodied being, that he was gifted with the ability to travel to Virdea. An ability many would sacrifice much for, but which would eventually destroy him.

It is/was also ironic that at this very second, a gate between Virdea and Bashful, Kansas, in 1960 was forming as a result of a miscalculation of a powerful wizard chasing his ex-girlfriend across time and space, and the changing wind pattern had caused an old branch to fall in the forest at the edge of Lark Field.

Thndry, who was now Nelson, regained his feet. Rndrl said, "Weather sense brother, we must regain the tree."

Ravens have a much finer sense of time than humans. For them, the world is over-cranked. Humans seeing through the eyes of a raven see those events in slow motion, a beautiful and dreadful feeling. Ravens seem very smart to humans because they have a lot of time to use the intelligence they have.

Nelson knew all of this from his previous visits and thus was able to take wing immediately and find a safe perch.

Now, that Nelson has shown up, I can turn the story over to his close third, because he really is a good narrator. He has a strong sense of visualization, an understanding of the moving pieces, and a way of describing complex scenes like he is making a cheap movie. Also, with all of the dialogue that will soon happen, my own omnipotent, fourth-person viewpoint will soon start to confuse the narrative; it may even create a time rift where no one can be safe, like what happens when you read Salman Rushdie while drinking too much Bénédictine. There is always that thing with having Cat Stevens on his ass unless a British court clears him of using the omnipotent fourth person, which is of course, my fault, not that of Mr. McKeeby or Mr. Rushdie.

I/Nelson huddled in the tree as the wind began to grow. I feared for my own safety and that of my brothers and sisters clutched to the sycamore, and that of all the humans I saw, heard, and sensed. Sensed was the term I used for the pressure detection matrix ravens have that provides a powerful form of perception. It came from air pressure being applied to a series of sensitive glands along the ventral and dorsal sides of the body. The result was a three-dimensional picture of the world that allowed a raven to track beings accurately, giving them literal "eyes behind their head." It was like having preternatural situational awareness.

Down below, the armies began to show the effects of the wind. At the outer edge of the cyclone, the peasant army was forced to drop their weapons, wrap their faces in their cloaks, and take a knee or be swept from their feet. In the center of the cyclone, the wind was picking up faster and faster, pushing armored soldiers down and breaking their formation. I could hear the Yellow King yelling angry words while officers used knouts to attempt to knock superhuman stability into the very human legs of their soldiers. Most of the soldiers regained their feet by locking their legs, but the columns were ragged with so many files kneeling.

Then a flash. Raven-vision showed it like a wipe splice in a film chain, a purple 1957 Chevy appearing as if from behind a big sheet like a hurtling steel bowling ball with pins flying in all directions. Only the pins were men in armor who just minutes before were prepared to massacre a field full of farmers for a purpose only an omnipotent mind could conceive. The car was traveling around a 100 km/h, fishtailing in the mud and bumping over the corduroy of warriors standing before them. The passengers of the car were yelling a purple scream of terror and exhilaration, as haunting, tinny music floated from a slightly cracked window in the rear of the vehicle.

The wind left so fast that objects being carried in it started to rain down onto the ground, robbed of the means of mechanical flight, while the Chevy skidded to a stop just feet from the Yellow King. Inside the car were three goggled-eyed humans. The human driving turned on window wipers and caused a spray of liquid to splash the glass pane in an effort to clean off the patina of blood that was coating it.

"We are not in Kansas anymore," one of the occupants said.

"No shit, Dorothy," said another.

The Yellow King was good at emoting. He was a huge man with no empathy and no feeling. Half of his soldiers lay broken like toys, while he was torn in a storm of a temper tantrum, pushing out to the universe a wave of hatred and yellow thought, "HOW DARE YOU." He raised his mace to bring it down on the Chevy, but it did not connect. Instead, the car accelerated rapidly then dropped into gear, squashing the most powerful monarch of the city- states of the western plains into a shape similar to that of a can of spaghetti dropped onto a sidewalk from a space station. Thus passed Rackhar Zil, the Yellow King of Virdea.

Two men stepped out of the Chevy, one in a worn leather jacket, and the second in an absurd charcoal suit that made him look like a bunch of triangles. A short-haired woman in a poodle skirt and a sweatshirt that said "College" got out of the back seat. "Nice work, Baby Driver, you fucking squashed the guy we probably had to talk to next."

The man in the charcoal suit said, *"Va te faire foutre,"* as he stepped gingerly around the twitching, metal-encased forms. The man in the leather coat went to the trunk of the car and opened it, revealing a transit case conveniently positioned for access. From the case, he took a rifle and a bandolier of ammunition, threw it to the man in charcoal, then grabbed a soft bag and a pair of medical kits.

The woman said, "Did you just tell me to fart on myself?"

The man who was Ivy d'Seille, born in 1928, caught the rifle out of the air followed by the bandolier of ammunition, which he deftly shrugged into. "Sure."

Around them, men in iron were regaining their feet. The ordinary soldiers had suddenly lost interest in participating in a massacre that was looking to go in the opposite direction than anticipated, at least their body language said as much. Not sure if the Yellow King was truly dead, the officers began to swing their knouts and try to beat some fighting spirit back into the men. The idea that their liege might self-repair and be pissed that the soldiers were not ready to fight was a horrible possibility in Virdea.

I (remember I am now a raven in the trees) watched the dance of the armored men with fascination, using my superior raven vision to take in the image like some super high-definition television picture. Their leaders wanted them to close in on the idling Chevy. It made sense because the odds were like a hundred-to-one still and the purple monstrosity was no longer positioned to make a horrific charge. Still, they held back. The result was something like an aquarium where everyone wants to see the great white shark from close up, but the glass holds everyone back.

Ivy said, "You think this lot is going to sit down and parley?" He was trying to get a helmet off one of the men who seemed to be twitching. The rest of the armor was flat like a tin can left on a railroad track. Useless.

Kelle replied, "Not now, we just pulped King Rat." She took the femoral pulse from where the armor did not cover and then shook her head. "You killed someone important, amigo. At least these red shirts seem to think so."

"I killed?" Ivy said.

<*Be calm,*> came a purple thought to all of their heads. <*This one who is now under my tires was not your friend.*>

The soldiers closed in a little bit. Rains-a-Lot broke open his revolver, caught the empty shells in his hand, and loaded it with fresh ammunition. From the soft bag, he took two canvas belts of ammunition in loops and wrapped them bandit-style across his chest.

Ivy ducked by the next man on the ground. He was alive but in shock. Ivy said, "Concussion, compound fracture of the ulna."

Kelle checked it. "Leave the armor on; he needs that set. Do you have Ringers?"

"Besides you?" Ivy asked.

"It is probably called Hartmann's solution," Kelle said with a sniff.

"Two bottles, more in the back, probably," Ivy replied.

Kelle said, "Give him one."

Ivy made the poke inexpertly and then used the cruciform hilt of a sword jammed into the ground to hang the bottle from, allowing the liquid to drip into the man's veins. Rains-a-Lot kicked him, and he looked up.

It was as if a dam was being pressed by more water than it was designed to hold. The soldiers at the back of the presser were being beaten by officers eager for them to attack and wanted to get away from that, so they moved forward in the crowd, only to reach a point where fear held them back. The result was a slow, turgid pedesis that the eyes of a raven were perfectly designed to detect. Ivy could detect it also, but only because he had been on the other side of such a movement.

"Get in the trunk," he said to Kelle.

"Fuck that, no one puts Kelle in a trunk." She ducked into the Chevy and started to rifle through her back-pack. Rains-a-Lot was shoving dead away from the car, creating a path of stable footing.

Ivy held up his rifle. "This is a Model 49 rifle. It has ten rounds in the magazine. I have five magazines, plus ten boxes of clipped rounds. Even if they all line up and walk up to the counter one by one for personal head shots, Rains-a-Lot and I cannot get them all."

Kelle pulled unusual things from her pack. A fire extinguisher painted orange. A plastic, yellow-and-black striped pistol. A strange little black handle. Then she shimmied into a strange cloth over-suit. Ivy brass checked his rifle. "Stay between us then." Kelle waved his comment away.

Rains-a-Lot pulled his hat down hard onto his head and grabbed Kelle by the shoulders. He looked deep into her eyes with a crease in his forehead. Kelle said, "Stay between you, got it, John Creasy?" He nodded and drew his pistol. She yelled as loud as she could into the air, *"Oculariatu s'ellu* ùn *vole esse sparatu!"* Then switching languages, *"Skrij,* če *ne? Eli? Biti ustreljen!"*

I opened my wings and said, "I wish I knew what she said."

"She said, in the tongues of the meadows, then of the plains, to hide or face death." Rndrl speared Nelson with his eyes. "Who now rides the wings of Thndry?"

"I am Nelson, the human," I said.

Rndrl genuflected with a daub duck of his head. "Nlsn, we honor your presence."

Another raven said, "This is not truly Thndry. Not in smell, not in form."

A second raven said, "It is man's work. A raven mind, but the gears of a human."

I looked at myself and beat my wings. "I appear to have gears."

"They work as well as flesh, and it means that perhaps our brother Thndry is safe." Rndrl said.

I danced a small raven dance of confusion. "The gears are not working."

Rndrl scolded me with a chirp, "They work, though they may be disrupted. There is meaning in you here, watch below!"

The crows in the trees were yelling, "Meat, meat," trying to egg the humans into fighting.

Rndrl squawked in anger and danced the red dance of anger. "The crows are a disgrace."

"What happens here?" I watched as Rains-a-Lot gently pushed Kelle between him and Ivy, as the two braced for their last stand. The green peasants took heed of the warning they were given and had retreated to the safety of the woods. The steel warriors were slowly gaining courage again to attack the newcomers and then destroy the children of the meadows.

Rndrl turned from the crows. "The green people, the farmers of the meadows, gather to fight the warriors of the plains to see who can have the produce and bounty of this land. With the Yellow King dead, run over by that purple priestess, I would think they would wait for a new King or one of the seven knights to arrive, but they are like crows themselves. Once the thought enters the mind, there is no room for a new thought."

A purple thought intruded into my head. <*These are my children. Help them please.*> I was a lot of things, but not schizophrenic. I barely had room in this raven brain for my own thoughts. An outsider was also present. I looked at Rndrl.

"It is the purple priestess who asks for succor," the lead raven said.

I could feel the sense of sadness for my own reasons. This was my story to tell just like it was their story to live. The story they shared seemed incomplete, though. This was not the end in Bolivia when Harry Longabaugh and Robert Parker shot each other in the head to avoid capture. This was not the last chapter in my last book, at least the one I wanted to write. It would be like if *The Wonderful Wizard of Oz* had Dorothy die of a brain hemorrhage right after meeting Scarecrow. Something had to be done! I was screaming in my own mind that the story would cease with the heroes dead on a pile of bodies in a magical land, dinner for impetuous crows.

"You speak their language?" Ivy asked of Kelle.

"Yep, been here, learned that, the t-shirt sucked," she chuckled when the joke fell flat with Ivy.

Ivy said, "Tell them to surrender, and we will release them back home."

She shrugged. In the language of the plains, she yelled, "You should run away, these guys are my sworn protectors, and my ex-boyfriend is a fucking wizard with a bad attitude."

Ivy asked, "What did you tell them?"

"To give up because you were a bad ass," she replied.

Rains-a-Lot chuffed. "I like Dorothy," he said.

The wind blew through my feathers as I watched with dread and said to no one a quote from the Darkfather, who does not exist in this timeline or story, "To be human with hands, to be able to affect history."

Rndrl twisted his body. "Who said one must be human to do a thing in history?"

I considered this. There was, to my knowledge, no book of the acts of ravens. The purple thinking on the edge of my mind said, *<History is only written by humans, Shaking Man, the rest of us can make it.>*

Kelle put her hands on each of her protectors' backs. "Guys, I think this is going to get pretty dry. Sorry we did not get to know each other better. Last question to ask is which one of you is going to be my Left Shark?"

Ivy laughed. "If I could ever figure out what you mean, I would have lived a great life. Rains, you ate Custer's heart, any suggestions here?"

"Ignore the taste," Rains-a-Lot replied.

I (Nelson, as a mechanical raven, keep up friend) turned my attention from the three doomed travelers and said, "Tell me Rndrl, how do ravens help create history?"

A score-of-a-score of ravens, the stock of the uplands, the great flight masters and mistresses, the long seers and the far speakers, the untrained corbies and the ancient lictors, stooped to listen to the ridden one that the purple thought had named the Shaking Man be declared the leader of the last conspiracy by the one who would become the greatest leader in all memory of raven-kind, Rndrl-Greatkind.

"I state that the Conspiracy of Ravens has been declared this the 4th Day of the Bear, 3684, and that our people shall see to the protection of the travelers as they tell their story in the land of Virdea."

The mass of ravens screamed in a terrible resonate, "Agree!"

The noisy crows yelling, "Meat! Meat!" fell silent, jittering in fear over an event no avian had witnessed since the days of legend.

"I say we will aid the Shaking Man who rides Thndry-god-touched, who is the disrupted gear of history. We will fly wing-by-wing, brother protecting sister, family joining family, clan to clan, and nation to nation in the black wind, the single claw of thousands stretching out."

Ravens hopped rhythmically in their own red anger, screaming as one being, "Agreed."

Kelle, Ivy, and Rains-a-Lot joined every living warrior, ranger, and peasant in the Lark Fields to stare in amazement as trees filled with huge black birds began to scream like worshippers in response to a chanter's calls. Ivy said, "Is that good?"

Kelle reached out to hold his hand. Kelle connected Ivy and Rains-a-Lot in a chain of touch, the lost sharing a minute of hope before they stepped off into the darkness of the unknown. She watched the yelling ravens shaking the trees and said, "I have no idea what that means; this is Virdea after all." She then dropped Ivy's hand and pointed at the soldiers. "They are scared as shit. Think they will run?"

Ivy shook his head. "Some people attack when they are scared." He scanned the cowering army and said, "You named this place Virdea?"

Kelle said, "Call it Oz if you must."

In the trees, Rndrl pointed his beak to the heavens and said, "Take wing, Conspiracy, and show the gods we are their children also!"

The dam of armored soldiers broke out in fear as ravens took wing by the hundreds and maybe thousands. The soldiers ran into a coordinated wall of invisible hell that washed over them like a tsunami, killing and wounding dozens even as they stepped out to the charge. I was not the best at flying, but the trick was in my brain, and I figured it out after a few missed wing beats. Falling into the formation, I figured out that it mattered when I beat my wings and where I positioned myself compared to the others. My brothers and sisters were ready to help as they gently made sure I sculled at the right time and stayed in proper echelon with my wingmates. Below it was a maelstrom of gunfire as the travelers faced the armored wave.

The Conspiracy flew in a great arcing circle, air slipstreaming us as our guidon feathers opened and closed to allow careful changes in ground speed. Once we achieved a good circle, we dove down in flights, letting our claws dangle low and barely brush the soldiers' helms. There was no way our sharp claws could penetrate man's steel, nor were they heavy enough to crash into a soldier as might a marauding eagle. Instead, each helm was lightly brushed with a ping, but hundreds of ravens were hitting each helmet, with a cumulative effect of a fearful distraction on the already spooked soldiers. I caught the trick of throwing out my tail feathers for tight control, using the slipstreams of my brethren to sustain lift and speed, then at the last minute using a slight loss of altitude to slingshot me back into the air where I could scull for formation.

Ivy was reloading his rifle from little strips of bullets as Kelle stepped forward with her extinguisher. She triggered the device, and it turned out to contain an orange liquid that sprayed across scores of the soldiers, making them scream and claw at their helmets. Each helmet that came off drew the attention of dozens of ravens pecking and clawing. I dove on a helmet-less man and found his head was covered in pepper spray, although I could not detect its heat.

Kelle was pushed back as Rains-a-Lot, and Ivy stepped forward to meet the first wave of soldiers. Here was the truth about guns—eventually, someone willing to pile bodies on the problem will win, and even trained, armored warriors were grist for the mills of ambition. Ivy was visibly counting down the shots in his rifle, while Rains-a-Lot had his Bowie knife out in his left hand, expecting to show the shades of his ancestors that he also could face his last seconds like a man of the plains.

A wave of arrows came flying into the first fascine of soldiers, staggering them and blunting the next wave. The Rangers had appeared from the forest and battalioned themselves into shooting groups, each group following the directions of a sergeant to create target zones around the travelers with both volley and targeted fire.

I saw the short reprieve this created, and I winged up to patrol the edges of the raven flights, keeping them out of the flight path of the archers, helping Rndrl form attack sticks, and arranging for a rotation of ravens to rest in the trees. In my head, I heard the purple thought, <*You are dying, Shaking Man.*>

No shit, I thought. So much for being born with a body that was a ticking time bomb.

<*No, it is Virdea that kills you.*> It was a counter-argument. I heard the force of the personality who wielded the argument, confident in knowledge.

I let myself slip to the side in the air, then ported to catch a group that was about to fly into an arrow fall, allowing my tail feathers to flange, throwing myself into a yaw, exchanging altitude for speed. *So who are you, purple thought?* It was odd speaking without voice.

<*I am Mama LeDeoux, hongoun Macumba of the Sacred Order of Petro, wife of José Gaspar, invested by the Lady Chaneli in the Christian year of 1811, and punished by the master Darkness in the year 1821.*>

That is a lot for a bird to remember. I ported then starboarded and caught a breeze for some altitude. "May I call you Violèt?"

<*Yes, although Violèt is more accurate, without the inflected e.*>

A flight of corbies burst from the woods, screeching that rest of the scouts were about to ambush the Rangers. I folded my wing and dropped to stand by the commander of the Rangers. He looked down at me, so I opened my wings and did the dance of surprise. In his tongue, he said, "Trouble, friend?"

I screeched, "Yesss!"

"Something coming for us?" Rndrl-Greatkind said.

"Trees!" I yelled.

He yelled, "Bronk, get ready with the gadget. Terl, on my command blow to receive horsemen!"

I took to the wing. Violèt said, <*Time does not flow here the way it does in reality. That is how magic works; the dimensions do not connect, not really. In my time, a windmill could catch energy based on the difference between the stillness of the mill and the speed of the wind. If time is energy, then this is all you need to know to understand magic and your own demise.*>

Way too much for a tiny bird to understand. In front of me, dozens of horsemen burst from the woods charging on the Rangers in an attempted *coup de main,* led by a brilliant warrior in cerulean cloth and gleaming chain. I tilted my wings up, losing speed and gaining a little altitude, then screeched, "Dive my brothers and sisters." I did not know if any were going to follow, but my raven sense said many who were hovering formed up on my tail and followed me in.

"Stay on target, Little Monsters!"

We dove as one, harrying the men and pushing them from their seats. As we regained our wing, a burst of arrows emptied a few saddles. Then the Rangers, seemingly doomed, dropped bows and lifted up long wooden poles sharpened on the end, while forest peasants rushed out of concealment with more of the primitive pikes. The horsemen reigned up and were felled and swamped by foresters who tied them up in jute wraps.

The purple in my mind said, <*No matter how smart, a raven is not a human, and your mind cannot survive spread across two brains. The part of you left behind is thrashing apart your body.*>

I came to light back in the sycamore. A young corbie screamed, "This is no longer Lark Field; the ravens have shown the world a new Conspiracy!"

Down below, the three travelers had stopped shooting as a surge of foresters broke upon them, pushing huddled survivors into wan clusters, disarmoring and disarming them, tying them into tight coffles of dejected ejecta. Kelle and Ivy again started to pull out and triage the wounded.

<*You should leave, Shaking Man, before you die on Earth. You will return, and the story will be told.*> The purple faded from my mind.

HAUTE ZOMBIE

DATE: OCTOBER 29, 1821
LOCATION: NEW ORLEANS, LOUISIANA PURCHASE

Violèt's most distant memory was of her mother, a dark and wise shadow, standing on the flaming deck of a slave ship. Before her was a dashing man, Armand d' Viteon, captain of the *Coucher du Soleil*, a pirate in endless wars of the New World. She knew her mother was important to her people; they had literally died freeing her from the chains of the slaver and getting her to the deck. The people, already doomed, spent their last seconds passing mother and daughter hand to hand, to a place where they might find rescue in the strong arms of the daring pirate captain.

And now, the three-year-old's eyes could see the flames burning down even this last chance to escape. Armand, holding onto a burning rope at the edge of the doomed slaver, reaching out an impossible distance, while her mother leaned over the flames, trying to keep Violèt out of harm, but also trying to lift her high enough for Armand to reach.

Just as it seemed too much, Armand made some sort of madman's choice. Choking up on the line he was holding, he leapt out and grabbed Violèt. As his arc passed back, he tried also to grab her mother, but the mother, not wishing to damage Armand's masterful swing, held her hands in and said, "Deou!" At the high point of his backswing, Armand released and went crashing into the rigging of the *Coucher du Soleil*, breaking both of his arms and both of his legs, but saving the young child.

Violèt had nothing in her possession, save a picture of a flower that would give her the name she would carry in her youth. The pirate though, honoring her mother's last words, called the child Violèt LeDeoux, a last name that was not unknown in the *Coucher du Soleil*'s homeport, New Orleans.

And now, so many years later, the story of how Mamma LeDeoux came to the City of New Orleans was lost in the mists of time. That girl who scrubbed floors in the Marin Ivre, a ramshackle bar at 131 Rue Royale, was no longer a person mentioned in the milieu of the city. Now, she was the Priestess who ran the Apothecary at 22 Rue St. Louis, an accepted figure in the mythology of the town, a name on the docks that held weight. She had connections to the Spanish and French eras and was a force both in the upper city and the lower.

Each evening, when the last client left, she would take the air of the Plaza de Armas and the Cabildo before sitting down at one of the coffee lounges along the edge of court district and ordering a strong sailor's coffee, taken noir.

October remained hot, the type of muggy, still heat that could poach an egg released from its shell. When the Americans had arrived, they had buzzed over the possibility of New Orleans. Maybe something could be done about the heat, the mosquitos, the streets, the levee system. It had taken them a bit to understand New Orleans resisted those changes just like it resisted all change. She was the Citie Grande Dame, an immortal woman who teetered at the edge of a great miasma, an ocean port from where the sea could not be seen.

When the Americans had realized that pirates roamed the streets side-by-side with the traders they preyed on and the navy soldiers who hunted them, it became obvious the old lady played to her own tune. It had no rules, but instead relied on traditions every bit as powerful. The one God, it was said, walked the daylight streets, but allowed the many gods their time in the shadows. And those gods were the masters of traditions that stretched back in some cases thousands of years to the great wizards of *Afrique*, the powerful *doctores* who called on the passengers and the messengers in ceremonies so powerful they could stretch the fabric of time and space.

Mamma LeDeoux represented that. Here she drank coffee, a priestess of the arcane powers, next to a coterie of priests from the Cathedral and a pair of priests from the Jewish Synagogue. A partitioner would pray at the church on Sunday, then visit Mamma LeDeoux on Monday to ask for her own special intervention to the powers. They could keep the daylight streets and the patronage of the new American masters. She would remain mistress of the night, a title no one had given her but that tradition deemed was hers.

It was one of those summer nights whose frisson could be smelled on the fetid air, driving away the languid, lazy feeling that the daylight hours gave one, and ushering in a sense of anticipation for events yet to occur. Time slowed in the summer nights, it became so slow in fact the distance between the aether and the real would stretch fine, and many acts impossible in the rationalism of daylight could be accomplished when the moon waned and the cicadas broke open in their nightly chorus that sounded like broken violin scratches.

Mamma LeDeoux's coffee came as she watched the nightlife begin to crawl out of its dayside holes. Legal students clerking in the halls or offices of law wore long black gowns, white powdered wigs from which sweat streamed in little rivulets, and carried sword canes, ever ready to thrash a rival whose rhetoric had become heated. Like fleet deer, the students were stalked by the better camouflaged of the prostitute trade, each dressed to appear like a barmaid taking a few hours to herself but willing to earn tips for the right "man of the world."

Sailors also plied the streets, released from ships coming from each point of the compass, with names on their caps like Torreon, Bay Harbor, Flamengo, Isluphur, and Sidris. Chasing the sailors were another set of prostitutes who dressed like high-class women that just happened to forget their blouses and panties, but who did remember to ship about three-times the makeup worn by the oldest society woman. It was the dance of the docks, where each side sought to fuck the other, but the fucking desired was so different, so nuanced, and worth watching as a visual sport if one remembered how hollow the actual act was. *Carnality became a time of magic in the wet August air*, Violèt thought. A timeless dance of commerce that no one would win, but that each might find a few minutes of pleasure, either in the release of sex or in the comfort of money that meant their starved bodies would not be found in the plaza the next day, to be thrown by the authorities into the bayou for the alligators to tend to.

Then came the pirates. Pirates did not wear their ship's colors or name on their uniforms, but they were noticeable if you knew how to spot them. Pirates on shore for pleasure wore outfits that even the most outrageous seraglio would not permit. Coifed women's coats were turned into dinner jackets, while brocaded wedding dresses became an outlandish set of pants. Dressed like a gang of refugees from the Sun King's court, pirates would turn heads on the docks. They were loud, vulgar gaggles of ringleted and rouged men who walked arm-in-arm like homosexuals in the District d' Rolane, comfortable to be touching their comrades because each had seen such things that were best forgotten when fighting for coin and reputation on the Florida Main. Instead of prostitutes, pirates were chased by small time vendors selling exotic perfumes, strange knickknacks, and bags of herbs, smokes, smudges, and medicines to make the pirate's life better at sea. Their reputation as great lovers with coin to spend and a strange desire for the softness of the touch of a woman also attracted a crop of young women interested not in their money but in the experience of being taken by a man of dual quality—a strong man who would weep in her arms and a man who knew where to touch a maid to send her desires mad—but who would take their turn as tigers-of-the-sheets, providing them pleasures they would never again experience as the wives of accountants or clerks in the halls of government.

The brightest cities of the Christian world could not provide a better night of entertainment then New Orleans at the docks. The sailors, soldiers, and other travelers all said it, the food here was eternal and different. The music was unmatched in its vim or verve, or in the fact that it could be reproduced nowhere else. Death may travel the darkest streets and claim a certain percent of the revelers, but those that survived knew they had lived.

As the sun fell and the bats started hunting bugs, there came people to her presence in the coffee shop. Now was the hours of her work. A young man whose love was being torn from him by a handsome rival asking for succor. A barrister that was losing a "must win" case as for a nudge. A woman with the canker caused by another Macumba wanted it removed and sent to the person who had hired it done. Each one came for advice and magic and left their coins when they were satisfied. All of them left satisfied.

At the end of her visit to the coffee house, Mamma LeDeoux walked back to her apothecary along the formerly roisterous streets lit by the flicker of methane. It was later at night, so the sailors who did not want to be chum had found themselves havens or were being beaten and robbed by the more unsavory elements of the town. One of the gangs of toughs approached her, but did not press the issue when they saw who it was they'd accosted. They were mostly stevedores anyway, and not one of the truly dangerous gangs, twisted men who murmured to the dark powers, which would raid the crypts for devil's ichor to mix with virgin's hair. The kids ran when she scolded them, knowing full well how painful and damning a case of the pox on their nethers was.

The night-covered buildings of the dockside stood taller than they did in-city, with gray walls of plaster and darker patches where ivy or even moss was starting to destroy the structure. All the city was in a constant miasma of decay that only the most vigilant could counteract. Her own apothecary was a business and a home. The bottom floor had three rooms, a kitchen, a presence room, a sales floor, and a parlor for guests to mingle. The second floor had bedrooms for her husband José Gaspar and her, the maid, and her rare apprentice, José's billiard room, and her own library.

As she entered her storefront, six shadows detached from the walls. A seventh shadow was sitting on her worktable.

"Well, what do you want me to do about he and him?" The one on the table was dead, and all of the six living were looking from her to what she thought of now as an object rather than a human. It was a valid question that Mamma LeDeoux asked of the six ill-dressed pirates. The man was about forty, with sandy hair, yellow skin—either from being dead a bit or from eating salt pork and not having good water or lemon juice for your toddies—and the half-lidded eyes that said death was as real as it smelled, the eyes that could not be faked by one trying to play dead. He smelled like a privy, cloyingly sweet, stinking, and feral all at once. He was also done to death several times with masses of small wounds that would collectively have equaled mortality for any human.

The man was lying on the table in her presence chamber that had seen other dead before, a myriad of dead whose loved ones wanted to speak with, or learn from, despite the expiration of life. The darkened room was lit by modern Argand lamps, but they were turned low-to-guttering and only a single tallow that Mamma LeDeoux had taken in from her study was truly providing light. The resulting shadows clotted along the walls, revealing only hints of what was there to be seen. The presence chamber of a Priestess of the Santeria Order of Petro Hodoun is a veritable education in the fetishes of magic. Beetles and snakes floated in silver jars of clear liquid while colored sand heaped high in bowls and small sleds. Trinkets in every metal and stones in many minerals stood on the shelf, some like the Florentines, the purple marble, and the hematite softly glowed in the darkness, as did some fungi and one dried fish.

"They let us take him after he died." The man was a salty, one of the dogs of the sea who spent their lives plying the ocean mains hunting great treasures. His clothing was straight jack from a ship's sea chest. Most of these buccaneers would rather go ashore disarmed than in jack that they had rifled from a slop chest. Mamma Ledeoux had lived about them since she was a child and knew their ways. She could read them like they were the political pamphlets that troublemakers handed out by the churches. These men were desperate and called by a higher power to do a thing they felt disgust for doing.

"Did they now, and what for?" she asked.

"Uh, we said we would bury him, but he whispered he had a message from your own José Gaspar. We thought you might want a word, you being as you are, no offense meant to the spirits and all." The man was stumbling over his words as his four compatriots looked on in horrified silence.

Buccaneers of the Florida Main were the last of a breed, picking up sailing jobs then turning to piracy when the sense of freedom found them through the humors of their liver, or maybe the gallbladder. Their days were numbered, and each year they looked more like hunted dogs to the dwindling list of ports that harbored them and ships that plied those parts. The day of the pirate was over, but these men had no sense of history and no way to know it had ended.

"And who is this?" she asked.

"He is William Mitchell." Nervous coughs filled the room.

She lifted a lid and peered into the man's eyes. "Englishman?"

"Yes, Mamma, by way of New York, you can hear it in his vowels when he speaks up and all tony. Begging your pardon, before he died, you could hear it." Vowels, Mamma thought. You heard that as well in the pirates of the Main. They were occasionally quite well educated, even when they hid this.

Mamma LeDeoux grabbed a storm lamp from her trove and lit it from a punk. It flared up, and she positioned its Cyclops beam on the dead man's face. "Now, just stop. Mitchell is the Captain of Gaspar's largest ship, the *Contedora*. How does he and him come to my drawing room and in death shop my wares then?"

"Well, there was this American ship, the *Enterprise*. The same one that done for James D. Jeffers you see, and that was okay because Gasparilla and Mitchell, they take on with Lafitte how useless Jeffers is, seeing as he has done for so many children and harmless women. So, *Enterprise* drags him back, or so we think, which lets us ply our little bit without that crappy packet crawling up our backside."

"Wait, you lot were with José Gaspar?"

"Since Tampa, Mamma, or so we all say that was our first prize worth speaking on." The man was acting like a reluctant child, lying to his mother by having her drag a story from him.

She grabbed a vial from her potion rack. It was cola nut extract—harmless. "Enough of this, I will be pushing this on you next, and you will be swimming in the agony of the damned until you say it all before me!"

The men who were all braggadocio and honey tongue on the dock, with talk of pikes and fists ever on their lying lips, backed down into the darkened corners of her home. They seemed to shrink five hands and deflate like a puffer fish accidentally dropped by its captor pelican. The leader of them, and maybe perhaps the bravest, turned his head and said, "The *Enterprise* ambushed us as we camped on Sanibel hiding our flint, you know, but Gasparilla, he fought them on the beach, and we had heard, died in the hands of the Americans. We came back and found old Mitchell cut like thirty fathoms of line with that pike hole in his throat, but he could speak. He said to get him back to New Orleans. We used canoes, caught a packet, and are back here, but William, he was dying, but said he had the words of José Gaspar as a message to you, and he would only tell it with the wind that passed his throat. Then, he died."

"The bastard!" she yelled, partly at the dead man and partly at her lover who would die on a beach for a misbegotten pirate crew with little a thought for those he left cold behind him. And now, to send this stinking flesh as his benediction.

And the benediction had left the postage due on his message unpaid. Mamma pressed down her purple dress and turned with sudden fury on the scrofulous leader of the water toads, grabbing him up into her hands and holding him like a rag doll, although he was six hands taller than she and stone upon stone heavier. "He said the wind that passed this throat. You are not making that up. Be careful how you answer because you three pay the bounty on this, and I think you know the bill is weighed in scales held by the skeleton princess."

"Mamma, truly, he said the wind that passed his throat."

"Do you know what that means?" Mamma got no answer and expected none. Pirates that cruised the Spanish and American mains, those that plied the pirate cities of New Orleans or Pensacola or Peneluna, the men who lived in the last generation of the free, all knew and respected the lore of Osta Fedoon, the practical religion of signs and acts. They knew that great practitioners moved quietly among them, learning at the feet of the Petro, the riders that exchange wind and sunlight for insight and power. They knew at least some of the teachings of Regla de Ochá, the prayers, spells, and supplications of the Santeria. They knew the "what and why" of the hidden society of the Macumba and could count among their acquaintances, many who used the charms of the Candomble, and the new teachers of the Umbanda. Though no book existed to say, "This is what and how." The pirates of the small oceans and shallow coves all understood, at least in theory, the jambalaya of religion, spirituality, and practical faith that had fashioned and shaped the worship of the small deities, the hidden spirits of human and animal kind.

Mamma LeDeoux was not called Mamma because she had children. Her faith in her husband José Gaspar had not overcome the mathematical fact that they rarely spent time with each other over the years until it was certain no children would come to them. She was called Mamma LeDeoux because she had mastered at least eleven of the thirty or so ways of understanding, which allowed her to, with clear conscience, charge people in her community for magic. She knew of herself as more than just a cheating witch doctor that poisoned a local well and then took coin to make people feel better. She knew the lore of dozens of African peoples whom the slave trade was busily erasing. She could repeat the stories of a hundred gods, knew the writing of the one God in his three-forms, and knew the ways to trick the lesser spirits, called loa, and entice them to do her bidding.

She put the scared pirate down and said, "The Venda, a people south and south again on the mother continent, have a type of healer called a mungome. They had a formula I learned for a liquid that would revive a man who was not yet dead a day, but past a few hours; the formula causes terrible changes. How long since he died?"

"Just as we came ashore. An hour maybe, if the church rings true in the darkness of the night."

Mamma tried to remember her Latin stages of death. Palor, they turn white. He was starting to show the grey of death. Livor, the body begins to sag. It is doing this. Algor, the body grows cool. She felt his head. It held warmth, some at least.

"We are on the edge. If we wait too long, the process creates a thing of horror. Even now, he will no longer heal correctly. He will have a shell of a life. By your words, it is his desire to deliver the message."

"You will not talk to his shade?"

She regarded the pirate. "The dead, they do not have to speak with us. This one says wind; he means speaking with wind. That is, using his own voice." She remembered the cola nut extract in her hand, swallowed a dollop, and said, "Get me that grey jug there."

Mamma took a painful hour to make the formula, to rub down the body with sand juniper, and to inject the stomach through the mouth with a concoction made from raw paw paw and Mexican peppers. Then, Mamma wrapped the body with copper wire fed into jars of saltwater heating on the fire and began to sing. The pirates joined in thinking it was a spell, but it was only a song from her youth, something to calm her humors. When the needed time had passed, she took the vinegar salt and splashed it on his nose.

The man shot up, screamed, and jumped from the table. "I am living?"

Mamma nodded.

"I am a zombie?"

"A manes-zombie." Mamma LeDeoux looked at the man with sadness. "With the wounds in you, and the time that passed, if I had tried to reanimate you, it would have made you into a horror. A walking dead man, you understand?"

"I saw it, in Cap-Haïtien, you understand, with a practitioner in Le Cap." The dead man stumbled and said, "I speak, I remember."

Mamma LeDeoux saw the man's friends cowering in disbelief. "You are almost William Mitchell."

"Almost?"

"A manes-zombie as I said. You and your essence are not infused in each bit of the body, but in your skull only. As long as your skull remains in one piece, you exist with whatever of your body is left attached to it to do your service. Your body does not rot, not when it is near the skull, but it does not grow either. You must eat, a little food with vigor, no vegetables. Heart muscles or brains are best to eat. You must drink a little fresh water. Nothing from the holy water font and saltwater is not your friend. If you had believed in the blessings of the water when you lived, the belief followed you into the unlife."

He danced a little. "It is as if I am my own puppet."

"Be careful, you and yours cannot feel yourself burn. Stay back from fire. Stay out of the sun. Do not freeze either. There are colonies in places of compromise, exotic, foreign places. Like Kentucky. And a manes-zombie, let us just say that while land creatures will detest your smell and avoid eating you, sea creatures will see you as delectable. A bass could eat your leg when you crossed a stream. Do not cross rivers except at bridges. And the ground is to be avoided. Sleep in bed, or you will get worms in your body. They like to eat eyes." She turned and got several small tins of salves. "It will be strange, but use lanolin on your skin, or olive oil if you can find it. Use this cocoanut salve along with the flesh of the juju plant. Aloe is your close friend. Anyone who grows a great deal of aloe likely hides a manes."

Mamma LeDeoux grabbed a dark bottle. "This is shea, essence of milk, and almond oil. It is for the hair. You will want to treat your hair as if it will never grow back because it won't. Buy a wig if it comes to that." She threw the containers into a travel bag. "This one is peppermint oil. Mint extract will keep bugs out of your body parts and make you smell less like a corpse."

"I cannot smell anything."

"You will not, ever again. You are lucky. Right now, and maybe for years, you just look like a man who had been terribly injured but by the grace of God survived. That will not be forever. When you finally decay enough, find yourself a coven with a protector, and stay there. Unless you opt to become an artifact?"

She braced him with her eyes. "What are you doing," he asked.

"Can you move?"

"No."

"Do not be scared. I am Marennla. That means, I am the one who made you, and I own your deeds, good or evil, and will face my own maker wearing your honor or dishonor. I am your 'O-ka-lima-nona, the thing that wields the monster in the night. Know that with a word, I could send you to hell. You have a message for me, then I will tell you your last truth, and you will never, ever, see me again. You will never return to this city. If you go to your pirate ways, you do that elsewhere. Understand?"

"Yes."

"Where is the respect, 'O-ka-mea-make?"

She could see the zombie-manes shiver, though it must have been affected. Zombies do not shiver. They do not feel cold. "Yes, Mamma," he said.

"You now have wind passing your throat, and you can see I did the best by you I could. You tell me of my Gasparilla."

"I fought by Captain Gaspar's side, and when I was near slain, dying I saw them overcome the Gasparilla, but they did not kill him. I heard their whole plan. They were going to have him condemned in Tampa City by the Spanish, but they are leaving their fort. We proved to the Tampans that it was a stupid place to build a city anyway, the tides favor the invader. It will be a thousand years people will remember our tearing down that town and putting it to the torch, years before anyone decides to build more than a trading post."

"Enough."

"Sorry, Mamma. It is pride you see. All of us who were there. The Spanish, they no longer admit there was a fortress or a town there. Erased from history by embarrassment. And the sailors of the *Enterprise*, they took Captain to Tampa not to be convicted, but to be condemned. The last act of a dying town is to kill the man that killed them, but they do not have to bloody their own hands. The *Enterprise* will patrol another month, they have said, then take Gasparilla to New Orleans to hang!"

Mamma LeDeoux was furious. It was illegal. No one in New Orleans would dare condemn the Gasparilla knowing how much sympathy and power the Lafitte faction still had in town. She could see the commander of the *Enterprise*; Lawrence Kearny had learned his lesson after tangling with Lafitte in Galveston. To have more than a Pyrrhic victory, he had to hang one of the legends. Captain José Gaspar was the biggest legend still living, if the rumors that the Spanish killed Lafitte were true. What other pirate was known to so many through rhymes, through impossible acts? The Spanish could try to make a city disappear, but as long as the great Gasparilla was the one who had put it to the sword, their attempts would be like whistling in a hurricane.

That meant fame to the man who hung him, and our little Lieutenant and the tiny schooner *Enterprise* were seekers of fame. "Tell me the rest," she said, her eyes locked on a jar that contained a fetal pig in preservative liquid, kept if she needed to perform the rite correctly.

"I stayed in the woods, and they ended up picketing Gasparilla near where I hid. He must have known I was alive and hiding there because he said in Creole I was to tell you they had him, the trick would work, but you have them, if you were willing. He said to choose the fastest packet and make him such."

"Stop. You and yours use exact words here now. Exact words. Your friends learned how important they were."

"Take the fastest packet and make him such. I am sorry Mamma; he was took away right after. It was only luck he communicated that."

She turned to the three pirates. "The *Enterprise* is close at hand?"

"I would bet sooner than later. It is more than a month, and she is not quayside this evening."

"And what is the finest ship at quay right now?"

The pirates talked among themselves, but there was little to contest. "There is a Fells Point built rum clipper, the *Maisey May*. She does tobacco as well. She is the likes no pirate can touch. Twelve, thirteen knots of the line in the less breeze, and out of it she can haul herself so close to the wind she might as well have two port sides. She had something like 400 tons as well, many of that in her length..."

"Enough." She took silver from a box on her Lutian cabinet. "I have tasks for you. You know what happens if you fail me?"

From behind her, the manes-zombie that was almost William Mitchell said, "They know what I will do to them if they fail you."

It felt as if a wind blew through the room, but the tallows did not shake or gutter. Mamma LeDeoux nodded and handed money to each one of the pirates. Calling them by their names, she said, "Fernando, you go to the old man named Chipper on Jackson Street and tell him I want a model of *Maisey May* by morning, but he must make it from one of the ship's actual planks. There is bribe money to accomplish that. Return with the model in the morning."

"Catoro, you go to the Jailor of the Police Jail. Pirates are kept with the slaves and away from regular prisoners. You tell him that five hundred dollars does not go far anymore and that we want him and his and his men warm. Tell him fifty now and fifty if we can speak with any pirate lodged in the jail before they dance in the square. You understand?"

She then turned to their leader, Beris. "You are a mate, are you not?"

"I am, Mamma."

"Then you dole out the rum and cigars, how can you do this?"

"If I cheat on the rum and cigars at sea, I will be keel hauled. That is..."

"I know what it is. Your back shows no sign of strolling the ship from the underside."

"I have never been hauled to, Mamma."

"I want rum and cigars for twenty people. I want two women for each of you from the Mistress Lestalie. I want food delivered here, now, for fifty sailors, whatever you have always wanted and never could afford. Use my name if they give you an argument."

The pirate looked at the manes-zombie, "Food and women for him?"

"Of course not. What use is that to his and him? Get some calf brains, a quarter stone is enough. Do not have them cooked. He will never again want a woman, unless he needs companionship."

William Mitchell said, "I am thrice married."

"And so three times you will disappoint."

When the pirates had left on their errands, Mamma LeDeoux turned to the manes-zombie and said, "You should leave, but here is my last advice. As you live, try to develop empathy, to embrace others. Close your eyes and try to feel the world without sight or sound. You can, if you try, develop a second sight. When you have that, and before you lose your body altogether, have a Macumba perform the right of the artifact on you. They will strip your remaining flesh and articulate your skull. The idea is you become an object with intelligence, and you can use your second sight to aid a person who is a master of magic. That is valuable; it makes you a familiar, so to speak. End up in a mortuary stacked with bones, and you will have an eternity of boredom that will rob you of mind and senses, unless you find how to release your own shade, and that may not be well either. Instead, you will be kept in a library, have a magic user to talk to, and maybe live many centuries in grace. Understand?"

He nodded. "Thank you, Mamma."

"I did it for Gasparilla."

As she prepared for the most dangerous moment of her life, Mamma LeDeoux considered pirates. She hated them and was always apologizing for them. They took to the seas seeking freedom and then found there was no freedom to be had without money or a boat. They took each, and many started with these British ideals of honor that no French or Spaniard would ever consider. They thought, with a boat, that they had become the people they despised, the lords in their carriage. When they touched land other than a pirate port such as New Orleans, they were cheated, treated as scum, their coins reluctantly taken, sex offered to them at a price, their possessions stolen as they slept, and they were beaten by town toughs protected by the leaders of the communities that only cared for them as a source of coin. Their freedom was an illusion in a world where their ports were falling to laws and forcing them to live on the edges.

Some of them, dejected fools, accepted it. They were free because they did no work but what they wanted. And they starved alone as weaker men plundered the plunderers.

Some of them, no better, snapped. They took to the seas and became feral beasts. They killed and maimed and stole without regard. Prisoners were tortured for no reason, then thrown to the sea with bets on what sort of shark would eat them first.

And pirates did worse. They arrived in town forty years or more ago, with cutlass and pistol, handsome and brilliant heroes with money. They persuaded girls to give them their virginity, then demanded their love, and expressed their own. Then, they left the passion behind for a life of men, austerity, horror, and pain. When the sea spat them back on shore, they were not the same boys who had left. They had rough hands and rough minds. A sound would make them strike out and break bones. They would yell in the night, and the candle of their love was extinguished. The young girl was now bound to a young boy who was neither young nor a boy.

Many women could console themselves with children, but if the young girl knew of a secret from her young boy, that he had returned very different, that he had left a stallion and returned a colt, then what could she do? Horse owners could call forth a stallion to service their dames, and no one need know that the service was done by another. But the colt would know.

And Violèt LeDeoux loved the colt, for all his faults.

So her children became the town. It took years of work and hard study to become a Mamma, a Macumba mistress of the deepest mysteries. She, the child of slaves, wore a purple dress of silk to walk out in every day, and the people of New Orleans accepted it. She was Mamma LeDeoux.

She was Petro, and was most often called to carry Erzulie Dantòr, although the little girl in her still wished she could have been chosen by Erzulie Fréda Dahomey. Still, she was satisfied to be favored by the powerful

Dantòr. Many slaves on the local plantations would call her Mai-Louise, while superstitious pirates would kneel and ask her for the blessing of La Sirène, and then ask for the protection of Agoueh, who was often assumed to ride Gasparilla as well as do her bidding.

Today though, she waited in her home and expected the word to come that her husband was here. And then, she would deal with Papa Ghede, and indirectly, fool Sanhedi himself. The three pirates let themselves in, their leader nodding. "The food, the drink, the women, the music, the smokes, it is all in the next room. Take as much as you like and more. Hurt the women or harm the house, and I will rip from you that which you fondle in the night." The pirates nodded and understood. The Mamma was generous but could punish.

It was night again, the time for ridings and spells. The pirates started somber, but it did not last long. How many of these benighted creatures are given a day where every pleasure, save self-respect and honor, is handed to them to consume as they wish? Mamma LeDeoux closed the door tightly. The raucous sounds of pirates taking pleasure was now muffled by the walls of Mamma LeDeoux's presence chamber.

Lamps did not gutter, but even burning colza by the pint, the room was dark and somber. On her table, now clean of everything except what was needed tonight, were two glasses of rum, a guttering tallow, two cigars rolled by freed woman in the open air, Aztec chilies, apple leathers, and a piece of Mother Earth, a lump of hematite the size of a man's fist. Something was hidden under the stone as well.

She lit the first, then the second cigar, and started to smoke. Then, she ate the chilies and the leathers, and followed it with acid hits of rum until her head swam. She closed her eyes and said, *"E hele mai i o'u nei akua o ke alahaka."*

Traditionally she would welcome the loa at the entrance to her mind and, in essence, hand him or her the keys to her soul. The loa would ride her to perform a minor task, sometimes simply enjoying the music at a party, and then they would repay the loan of her body with a boon of knowledge. This time though, as soon as the loa settled in, she reached under the hematite stone and pulled out a pair of carnelian earrings, each with a spray of tiny amethysts. The combination was an unforgivable sin usually found on death masks to trap the soul of someone, keeping it around to question by force. Worn as earrings, it trapped the loa.

"I do not understand my daughter." The loa's voice pierced her mind with a low, resonate tambour.

Violèt steeled her inner mind and told the Loa, "I am in need of your powers, and I do not have anything to trade you."

"You stole a soul tonight daughter, I know this, and I understand it. You had my blessing and still have it." There was a curiosity there. A desire to understand her endgame.

"I steal another," she said.

"You may have a hundred," he replied.

"I steal that of José Gaspar." There, she said the finality of her request that was a demand. She intended to do the unthinkable and unspeakable and force a loa into the contract. She was damned.

"Sanhedi will never permit this, my daughter." His voice had a rising tide of anger as he realized the enormity of her crime.

"Not of me." She confirmed his fears with three words.

She could feel the spirit of Papa Ghede prowling her mind. He had gone from kind and loving to something like a caged panther that José had described to her at his bastion on Sanibel. "He does not love you," the loa said.

"He is a pirate. He loves no woman." It was true that pirates loved women, yet did not love them. Rather they adored women and treated them as their treasure, which could mean burying them on a deserted beach in some foreign island.

The loa was brimming with anger, but it could only be detected by spirit stuff, not by the tone of his voice. "He has children. In Spain, from a woman named Sanibel, who he shared with his first mate Rodrigo."

In her mind's eye that hurt, but weakness was failure. "He is a pirate, did I not say?"

"You are not his mother?" It was almost a question and almost a statement.

Clever, clever loa. "Am I not?"

The loa conceded, "You are a Mamma."

There were seconds of empty space and time to consider. She reached for the rum and poured another large glass. She took a large drag from the cigars, both at once, and then tossed back the rum.

"Thank you for that." The loa was happy, even in his prison, to taste human rum and smell human smokes. "I am sad because you will be punished. Let me ask you, do you know what will happen to Gasparilla?" Then he said, "Have you fully considered what Darkness will do?"

Darkness, the horror that guarded the interface. She had detected though that in recent years he was changing, becoming softer, more understanding. Best ignore Darkness until he strode into her presence chamber. Instead, she said, "His soul will be translated into a ship, and he will sail the seas for as long as men float upon water. I suppose one day he will wreck, and then he will be part of a beach somewhere, but this is what he wants. He has always wanted this."

"What about you?" the captive loa said. He had noted she had ignored his reference to Darkness.

"Punishment, perhaps?" She laughed at the understatement.

A time of emptiness again. "Gasparilla will not only pay with his life, daughter, which is lost anyway, very soon, but he will pay with his fame. He will go from a figure of history, like Julius Caesar, to a figure of myth, like Robin Hood. His greatest exploits will be forgotten. The meaning of what he has done and why will be lost. If he exists, it will be as a fairy tale, a thing of myth. Can the vain Gasparilla, last of the buccaneers, really want this? He has spent the majority of the magic he owns building a reputation, the last of the buccaneers. Now though, he will disappear in time."

"He says he and his do want this, do I to question the desires of the Gasparilla?" She looked at a mirror, seeing her own reflection. Gone was the child who had bedded the most famous pirate of the main and won his heart. The woman who remained was so much more ... and less.

"This will be done, but I predict that you will not find your punishment too hard nor will it last forever. And maybe people will remember Gasparilla, like a dream, a shadow of himself."

She hurried into the night. There were many things yet to accomplish.

SEVEN SPIRITS OF THE YELLOW KING

DATE: 9TH DAY OF THE BEAR, 3684
LOCATION: LARK'S FIELD, GREAT MEADOWS, VIRDEA

Raging storms, evil gods, ruthless demons,
who in heaven's vault were built of coal and flint,
fire-breathed by wizards chained to altars
azure on cobalt spires,
To serve the Yellow King on the sunshine throne.
A whistle of death fills iron muscles with krakle,
as armored heads lift from granite slumber,
burning opal eyes flashing duty bound to track
beings of flesh, and harry the guilty
through green fields and darkened days.

Seven there are, South Wind and Cursed Dragon,
Bone Knight with Fire-Touched Wolf,
Vengeance Lighting and Blood-Soaked Beryl
Led by terrible Lord Shibbula the confounder.
They walk in twos from city to city in

flashing clouds of storm,
called forth on yellow quests, to hunt the terror fled,
riding wind twists dark and pregnant will ill affair,
an early dusk presaging terror filled night,
and a slipped morrow-mirror.

Rzdr was a brave corbie; a child of the upland ravens. She was free to fly the wind and unencumbered until she found a mate and joined one of the societies that ruled each creature's totemic life. And now she was sitting above a battle starting the long journey into timelessness, waiting for lost bones to be stripped, metal to rust, and clothing to molder into random entropic soup.

It was then that she saw the flash. First one, then another horseman appeared from the darkness, vomited out from the void like sour fish cast forth to ease and grace the passage of the rest of the meal. And she immediately knew who they were. They were the seven umber knights of the Yellow King, drawn to their monarch's death like crows to a week-old raccoon body, late for the party but still with the eternal desire to lord over a lost being by dominating their remains. There were Ventus, the South Wind, and Mussiùdragu, the Pain Worm—the first with the symbol of the blowing breeze on his shield and the second with the tortured dragon in manacles, face blowing smoke to the sky in impotence. Then there were Devitu d' Cavallu, whose shield was a pattern of locking bones, and Lupufocu, with the image of a burning wolf. The stark red lightning bolt showed that Viddigatura had arrived with Rossusangutu: the prince of the blood-soaked gems.

Six were present, and Rzdr watched with dread as they lined up like side boys and prepared for the seventh, who always traveled in ceremony. It was said among the ravens that Lord Shibbula the Confounder knew only the ways of death magic, and where any other being who traveled the gates used nature, or study, or sheer will, Shibbula powered his being with the blood of innocents. The gold-red of a human-made, magical gate opened in the charnel field and a beautiful woman in a white dress wearing oak leaves about her brow stepped through, leading a great white horse with metal barding. She immediately fell to her knees and began screaming in agony as her soul was sucked from her being. Then came two commoners in grey and brown burlap outfits and jute sandals, each holding sprays of green commonweald. As they had stopped, each burst into horrible flames and screamed as they burned, their human tallow forming the fuel that would keep the oakum-like material they carried lit like giant candles for hours, casting bright, green-tinged light on the field. And finally, two more commoners came through, each holding the hand of a man who stood tall above the rest, dressed in a great bath of steel armor and armed with a great mace known by all as the *testa di morte* that which stalks death in the shadows. As he released the handgrip of the two that lead him, they screamed as if gut-punched, and their deaths closed the shining gate.

"The King is dead," Shibbula said with a deep, booming voice.

"The King will live!" the others screamed.

"Behold, the King is carrion," Shibbula replied.

"We avenge the King!" came the reply.

Shibbula seemed for a second cast in doubt. Birds can read human doubt, at least ravens can. Seagulls will never steal the bread of a confident person. They will always get those that doubt. For ravens, the skills came with dealing with men. A doubtful man is a dangerous man. A questioning man is wise and safe. An all-knowing man will destroy everything in an instant. A confident man can change the world with a single action. It is no wonder that ravens want to share their wisdom with humans.

Here Lord Shibbula was doubtful, and the raven could almost read his mind. The Yellow King was not a man. The Yellow King should be a person of great power. When the previous King dies, the Knights ride together as one on a quest, at the end of which something concrete is returned in triumph to the city-state, and the people are introduced to the new Yellow King who is the standing lord. The exception, though, is when the Yellow King is murdered. To assure that none of the Knights murdered him, they ride forth as a group seeking to avenge the King's death. Whoever then kills the King's killer becomes the new Yellow King. Like a horrible game made real by the rules of Virdea.

Rzdr had to report. A crow was sitting on a branch, peering with a worried eye down at the fires burning unnaturally in the field below. It changed its gaze to her and asked, "Meat?"

Rzdr considered. "Eventually everyone is." Then, she took wing.

Considering the danger that existed in the glade, Rndrl Great of His Kind was depressingly close by. They were sitting in the branches of several great paw paw trees above a crowded encampment of humans. There was a drowsiness about the whole scene as humans feasted on late pau-apples, great hunks of salted pork, barrels of dun-biscuit made from the ends of summer wheat, and what looked to Rzdr to be deer meat, the choicest offal from which was placed politely before where the ravens roosted, allowing her brothers and sisters to swoop in safely for a bite. A water barrel also showed the respect of the humans for their brethren, as finding water was one of the most time-consuming things. They could endure with little water, and the duties of a conspiracy caused many to forego simple pauses for water. It was a kindness.

Rzdr landed next to Rndrl the Great and the Ridden One who was being fed carefully chewed deer liver. Rndrl, always the wise teacher of a corbie scout, saw Rzdr had landed by him and said, "Riders generally are not good at eating or defecating, so we must feed our brother each chance we can."

Rzdr danced acceptance of the wisdom and opened her wings as a sign that knowledge was taken in like warmth. Rndrl was truly the great of their kind. She said, "The Seven Riders of The Yellow King are in the field of slaughter. They will take scent soon enough."

Rndrl the Great chewed more liver for he-that-was-Thndry and fed the ridden the moist gobbet as if he were a fillet in his parent's nest. "They will seek the new King."

"They seek revenge against that which our conspiracy is called to help."

Rndrl danced in surprise and cawed. Then, he yelled, "Seer!"

The Speaker, eldest of the wind, landed by their side and genuflected to the ridden one and Rndrl. She was old but spry, and her mind was like a crackle of fire in the silence of the forest. "Beloved," she said with true warmth and wisdom.

Rndrl genuflected and said, "The Seven Knights of the Yellow King."

"They will be seeking the new Yellow King once the body of the old has been found."

"They will quest far for their answer?"

The Speaker danced a dance of shame and bent her head. "I should have thought of this, no, the new King is that who slays the killer of the old King, when the King passes by violence."

A purple thought came upon them all, a gentle warm nudge in their minds. *<That is I, my children.>*

It had taken them time to accept that the purple object of straight lines and odd color was a being, Rzdr thought. The humans, they could tell, responded to her with varying degrees of affection, but not the affection of a living thing. Thus, they did not truly know their object was magical, let alone sentient. Not that each did not carry some magic in complete ignorance of the object's importance. The little glowing box of the woman named Kelle. The silver pistol of the man who makes rain. A charm around the neck of the man named Ivy. The children of men knew not what they held until it was lost. A raven corbie, such as Rzdr, could look at such magic with hunger. Sometimes the desire to own magic was so great, one could violate the laws of the clan and steal some small object to hide in a nest like a warm rock left to heat the children as they busied themselves with growth.

Rndrl stopped their racing thoughts. "We must warn the travelers of their need for flight. Rzdr, fly and face the challenge of the hatching!"

Electricity ran through Rzdr. The challenge of the hatching was a test of maturity in any raven's life. It was the reason the gods allowed your shell to open and permitted you to push beak and talon through to the warmth of the world. It was the reason you were born raven-smart instead of crow-dumb. If you were sung about in future years, it would be the challenge of the hatching that led you to greatness and memory, or failure, and a worse memorial. She stretched her wings again, then genuflected, power charging her young, strong body.

The Great Raven loomed above her and said, "There is an object on the Seven, something that in the hands of a human below us would yell 'flee!' I cannot know what this is, but you will when you return to steal it. Take wing now, and bring what you find to the humans, Ranger Lord and Traveler Mistress. GO NOW!"

Maybe there is a need for a fourth person to describe the flight of Rzdr. Ravens are unusual for birds. Most birds are mimics. This meant that a large part of their brain is designed to copy that of the birds around them. In that way, they are not much different from humans I suppose. When one bird takes wing, thousands will take to the air never thinking about why they have leapt into the sky, never wondering if this was the right thing to do. Ravens only have a little of this instinct. When ravens of the same clan act, they will instead seem to trickle into a flood of movement. First one, then two, then twenty taking flight, landing to peck the ground, making some noise, or other.

This is that everyone has a duty, and that duty is not the same. Rzdr, on the wing for an impossible job, was dedicated to one thing. As word spread that the conspiracy was preparing for action, scouts would slowly take to the air to determine if danger was nearby, warriors and hunters would defecate and drink one last gulp of water, corbies would escort expectant mothers to food and then off to their hiding places in their forests. Seers would gather, then disperse to share information, and messengers would take short flights to stretch their muscles. To a human, it appears to be chaos, but to an educated and omnipotent observer, it is like watching the Milos Forman movie *Hair* and realizing all that crazy gymnastics are actually a syncopating scene of surreality fed and being fed by reality.

And Rzdr flew until she found the Knights of the Yellow King torturing a peasant. The theory, she knew, was a flawed one. No peasant will tell the truth until, in the words of Little Bill Daggett, "You hurt them not gentle like, but bad." And bad means in a way that the torture victim knows will forever change their life. Rzdr did not realize in her mind the depth of cruelty that humans can visit on another. She was about honor, and fun, and exploration, and filling the pangs of hunger, and maybe someday, the warmth of eggs and the demands of the next generation on her.

The humans who now stood in Lark's Field were about exigency. They were permitted a level of actions that lesser beings might consider evil because they lacked the time to act any other way. The peasant they caught trying to steal gold from the bodies of the slain was a vessel containing only one thing they cared for: knowledge. The vessel, however, was flawed—as all humans were—in that the information they had was tainted by the lies that went along with being a member of the lower social orders. The crafty pervasiveness, the halting obedience, the prevarications that made any sentence a slope of deceit, could only be cleansed by the burning fire of pain. Pain, not that of wounded muscles that would quickly dim but the psychological pain that said you were forever mutilated by the questioner, could be mutilated worse, to live your life in howling agony: sans fingers, missing toes, with both ends of the alimentary canal forever damaged and painful to use, with genitals destroyed, killing the promise that most peasants hope for, no matter how terrible their life, and that is a chance at futurity.

The peasant in question was Howvard, a candlemaker and dirt farmer who had recently left his parents to till the land of a vacant steading, raising bees, flowers, milk, and if he did well enough, he hoped to attract a wife to his side to form a family. He was not perfect. He was vain: his hair a beautiful shade of black and his skin being kissed with a deep copper that the lighter-skinned people of the Meadows saw as exotic and beautiful. He was not as honest as he could be, having at times helped himself to goods he knew belonged to others. He was also quick to ignore warnings of danger, which is why he decided to glean the remaining slain despite being warned that Will O' Wisp and Jony Jump Up would be coming for their share in the darkness. His faults, though, had not caused him to deserve being tied naked to a tree by seven angry knights and put to the question in racking torture. However, to quote William Munny, "Deserve's got nothing to do with it."

Rzdr flew into the horrible tableaux and failed to recognize what one human was doing ever so carefully to another human being with a small flensing knife. The deft cutting was causing sprays of light blood to fly up and spatter all the knights. Lord Shibbula, helmet removed, was at times wiping his face with a monogrammed silk cloth, the letters *SR* entwined on the blood-stained fabric in complex curlicues. It was this bit of fabric that Rzdr saw as her message, and I believe she chose correctly. Bald eagles can carry their own weight if they have good aerodynamics and the right approach planned, allowing them to maintain airspeed until they catch an updraft of a thermal. Rzdr was nowhere near the size or lifting wingspan of a bald eagle. Massing little more than 1 kilogram and having a wingspan of a meter, she was proficient in snatching mice and voles that mass around 20 grams from their hiding places in tall grass sangers in open fields. Unlike the great eagles, the largest of which tips the scales at 9 kilograms, her feathers made little noise when she dove. Instead, she controlled her downward flight when hunting by a process her brothers and sisters called "pouching," the subtle change of aerodynamics of her leading and trailing edges by the flattening or raising of feathers into the air stream, a process so subtle that even today scientists have not detected it.

Even a mouse could not hear her coming out of the wind, and seven men torturing a screaming eighth would never notice. It was graceful to watch the brave corbie as she saw her opportunity and took wing, porting into her wind pocket, pouching her feathers until they provided both lift and speed, flexing her clawed feet to act as both subtle dive breaks and to catch her willowy target. She puffed her chest once, bringing into her brain a raft of data from her body, generated by pressure-sensitive spots on her body. Then she dove.

Now, as an ironic consideration, I would have had her dive right into the claws of her extraordinarily powerful and menacing-human foes and had this scene end with her tied up next to the human undergoing an eschatological fandango of pain.

Instead, she dove with all of her skill and all of her heart, and she snagged the bloody strip of silk, then rose into the air in exultant pride. With that, it is time for me to pass the point of view baton—like an ethereal talking stick—on.

Kelle looked out at the cheering crowds. So often in the last years, she had expected death, and so repeatedly, she had been snatched from the jaws of the reaper, she had lost track. And now her ex-boyfriend, who was both a major stalker pain in the ass and one of the most powerful wizards in two universes, was chasing her through the multiverse. It was hard to claim her problems were ordinary.

The crowds were happy, but here and now, they had 372 problems, the survivors of the battle of Lark's Field. In the here-and-now Virdea standard, the people of the meadows were ready to slaughter the lot of them. Worse, Ivy and Rains-a-Lot seemed ready to agree.

Kelle tried to channel Ursula K. Le Guin. She would know exactly how to handle this. Sadly, aside from considering gender transformation, a magical possibility that Virdea made possible when using a portal, or learning the true name of a dragon, which Virdea had a few of, most of whom did not hang out in human lands waiting to be commanded by clever scholars, she did not immediately think of anything.

"Let them go," she said, which was the limit of her clever arguments.

Ivy and Rains-a-Lot did not hear her. They were tied up in a minute discussion of bartering for provisions. Tired of being ignored, she pulled an air horn from her pack and triggered it, causing a long, loud blast of sound to issue forth from its bell. The camp became as quiet as a cemetery on Monday and all eyes turned to her.

For a second, she felt incredibly self-conscious, like when that asshole handed around to her college mates a rather risqué video she had made. Things being what they were, she was bound to see it and to feel incredibly betrayed. She had the last laugh, though. No one knew that a student in a master's program could be jailbait, but the feeling of eyes on her made her stomach do flops. After the silence stretched, she said, "Let them go."

Ivy walked up to her as though she were an errant child. He was a handsome man with a facial scar and muscular like a greyhound with spiked hair and an angular face. He did not wear a beard, but instead, he seemed to always be a week shy of shaving. His English was masterful in some ways, with an Alan Rickman brogue that hinted he was from somewhere exotic when in reality he was just a kid from Hammersmith. Despite this, she had heard him curse in French and imagined he was some child of the former French Empire, a Beau Geste-like adventurer who had seen the exotic lands of sand and jungle in the service of his colonial power. His eyes burned blue like icy fire, and he had a haunted, forbidden cast to his continence. "Dr. Brainerd."

"Kelle," she said firmly.

He nodded. "Kelle, things are different here."

She looked around in an exaggerated fashion. "Really? And how often have you visited Virdea?"

He stopped and stared at her.

"What language are they speaking?" she asked.

"Some sort of Italian," he replied.

"Corsican. I happen to be fluent. What is the common practice for captured soldiers in the city-states?" He stood silently. "Well, you're right. They tend to slaughter them, maybe with a little torture and some public frivolity, but that does not mean we have to be barbarians."

He looked pensive, like he had underestimated her authority. "You propose to let them go?"

"And give them some food. And get some clothing from the pack train. Maybe offer the ones that want to work the harvest a chance at staying here for the season."

Ivy raised an eyebrow but motioned for her to take charge of negotiations. There really was no trick to it. The people of the Great Meadows were kind with no military guile except for the cunning Rangers. The question was the soldiers. Were they the brand of fanatic killing machine the Yellow King used to prey on the weak, or were they the more mercenary professionals that would refuse an offer of farming but would happily run for the lowlands if given the chance? Or maybe, were they just farmers caught up in a war they did not choose? She walked over to the huddled men, guarded by serious Rangers wielding deadly yataghans and serious-looking bows.

She had to give this one to Ivy. He had established a triage and treatment for the wounded. That was a pleasant touch of the twentieth century in him, but how many people could they treat with the medical supplies they had, and how much skill did they really have at plucking forth bullets from the grievously wounded? Many would die, but their agony was being seen to by the Meadow folk in what fashion it could be. It was obvious to her that those soldiers who had surrendered while still healthy could see that. They could also see the great mounds of food being eaten with little being given to them.

There was a single man whose aura glowed purple, a glow only she could obviously see. Kelle was forever being surprised by magic, and although learning it was incredibly slow, she was not dense. This man was who to talk to. She mustered up her courage and walked up to him. At her back was Ivy, with his scar and serious-looking rifle, and Rains-a-Lot, whose athletic form and stern countenance could scare a professional wrestler out of his lunch money. She thought sillily that it made a girl feel kind of warm to have men such as these just assume protecting her was their duty. It had been a long time since she felt this way, in control and alive.

"You!" she said to the purple glowing man. He started. "What is your name?"

"Centurion Bastian Blave." A purple thought made her feel this was a lie.

"Did I ask you to lie? Many people here want to treat our prisoners in the same way the Yellow King does his own captives." There was a quailing in the ranks of men. The Yellow King loved to take soldiers who surrendered to him and ask them for their eternal allegiance. He did so after impaling them on a stake. If they gave their eternal allegiance, then they would be given water as loyal subjects. Nothing though would get them off that stake, and when they grew tired enough, they would slip down onto it, killing them. For its beauty, Virdea had some real evil lurking about it.

"I am Master Centurion Kull."

Correct. She nodded at the man and stepped right up next to him. She heard a hiss from Ivy and saw he was sticking a knife onto the end of his rifle. Kelle had no idea who invented the bayonet, some clever Frenchman, but it was such a silly, useless little thing, a knife on a deadly rifle. There was probably something Freudian about the things that Kelle was bound to miss. Like, "Here, I have a penis on my rifle, so stay away from my woman."

She turned back to Master Centurion. He was older with grey-tinged, short hair, a rectangular, handsome face, piercing eyes, and the beautiful mocha skin tone that said he was likely from the Deltas originally. His accent said he probably spoke the lilting and musical language of that land, but except for the phrase, "*L□y tay ra kh□i mông tôi,*" which indicated a desire for a trader to keep his hands off her ass; she was not even sure if it was an Earth tongue at all.

Lowlanders rarely used phatic language in conversation; it was considered condescending. "Do you have an opinion on what we should do with you?"

He bowed. "I do not know your name." It was a statement of fact, inviting her to tell him whether she desired polite conversation as equals.

"Doctor Kelle Brainerd. Brainerd is my family; Kelle is my designate."

"Then by the people of the Meadows, you would be Bonnadonna Brainard di grande impurtanza. I bow to you my *nhà tù*."

"He just called you a jailor."

Kelle turned to Ivy. "You speak the trade tongue?"

"No, that is Vietnamese."

"You traveled in Vietnam?" Kelle hit her head mentally. Given his age, Ivy could have lived in Vietnam or even fought there.

"I spent my time at *la rue sans joie*."

The street without joy, she translated in her head. What a fucking piece of work is mankind to accuse a place of being without joy when it was only man who could truly control that. "Whatever, keep an ear out for the tongue being spoken; I do not know it." She turned back to Master Centurion. "I am your jailor. I have a very short time to determine if I shall be your executioner. We have a few options. We can strip you and drive you into the woods."

"Where we will die," the centurion said grimly.

"If that is the will of the gods, then it is their will." Kelle saw him laugh at that one. "We can take your manumission and provide you all that is due a free guest leaving our lands in peace: food, water, shelter, and directions."

The centurion nodded. "I am not sure you know who and what is likely chasing you now. They may chase us as well. The knights of Carkoza do not forgive a defeat by the soldiers of the land."

That line made Kelle fearful, and she racked her brains. What did the poem say: *fire-breathed by wizards chained to altars azure on cobalt spires.* God damned, she hated poetry. In college, it seemed like a great way to get out of having to write for real in creative writing class. Discard some profound couplets about grief, and the professor would shit herself, leaving Kelle to get to real studying about the interaction of quarks and the mathematical models of strange and up, so frustrating and beautiful in their asymmetrical symmetry.

"If anyone is willing to take oaths to a family group, the Rangers, or to me personally, then we can arrange for you to be hidden and fed." Ivy chuckled, as if this arrangement might be hard to sell to the thousands of Meadow folk who only a few hours before were ready to die at the hands of these men, but she had already spoken a little to the leaders. They were transfigured in a metaphysical awe over the people who they called "the Travelers." There was the brave fight against all odds, the amazing mechanical beast that seemed to be under their command, and the strange behavior of the ravens who, even now, sat quietly staring at them from the trees as if waiting for another shoe to drop. Kelle knew that she was speaking for the people. Even the purple feeling confirmed it.

Master Centurion said, "I and mine will take an oath to the Bonnadonna Brainerd di grande impurtanza such as we never in our lives did the Yellow King. We will take the two-sided oath that says we protect the other, and harm to the other is harm to us. We are serf and mercenary, accepted as citizens nowhere, but where you command, as long as you remember your own oath, we shall stand."

Oaths mattered in Virdea. They were magic, even the least of them. Citizenship was rare in the city-states, which was why rebellion was common. A citizen spoke an oath that was only as powerful magically as the oath the leader of the nation spoke in return. Kelle looked out at the field of men and saw most were glowing purple now, caught up in the magic.

It was the dead. Necromancy brought power.

If you killed just for that power, you were a blight on the world. If you stood where death occurred and found a way to peace, the magic could be thrice as powerful, and be wholesome and good.

She felt Rains-a-Lot step forward, knife in hand. For a second, she feared violence, but instead, the stern man took the blade and cut his left hand. He then stared at Ivy. Ivy said, "For fuck's sake. Really?" It was just a second of that hidden bond that Kelle had seen existed between the two men. The fact they rarely spoke but seemed in tune with each other. Ivy slung his rifle, pulled a lock blade, and cut his own hand as well.

Blood magic was a spontaneous gesture by her guardians. Necromancy, from the dead and dying, to see peace brought to them. *This is powerful shit,* she thought. The purple intrudes into her thoughts, unasked for but gentle, like the feeling her long-lost mother gave her when she covered Kelle with a blanket as she hid in her closet. Without knowing why, she reached her hands out and held the unwounded hands of Ivy and Rains-a-Lot. And she knew from her ex-boyfriend's books, that this was a binding ceremony, an oath-promise. She felt a hush in the field as thousands of Meadow folk fell to their knees.

Master Centurion came forward and said, "Bonnadonna," then kissed her cheek. Then, each one came forward. Those without the deep-purple aura hesitated, and Kelle shook her head. They were gently led away. No one needed to say to treat them with mercy.

The Rangers stood tall and silently as man after man, formerly enemies, came forward and touched or kissed her. The commoners, condemned to death, now sang a song of hope, newly written, about the battle of the ravens. And when the last of the soldiers had taken the oath, a brave raven with a bloody silk cloth landed in front of her and screeched.

The ravens in the trees were beginning to fly like their massed forms were part of a single twirling dervish, like each of them had been taken over by a spiritual ecdysiast who demanded that they must now leap to the air in a magically fed hurly-burly, churning the air with their wings like a blender making a magical mai tai. Each bird had suddenly decided to take on the role of spiced rum, coconut rum, grenadine, pineapple juice, or orange juice, and leapt to the sky simultaneously when an unearthly hand pressed the "blend" button. All but a single, screeching blackbird and her bloody pocket square. The lead Ranger, Sigurd, took it and said to Kelle, "The King's Seven are among us. We must flee!"

"What do they want?" Kelle asked.

"The one who kills you becomes King in Carkoza, the great city-state of the Yellow King." The warrior looked over as Rains-a-Lot brass checked his pistol. "I would not count on your wondrous tools working against them."

Ivy was watching his partner. "Rains-a-Lot thinks it is better than letting these people kill us without fighting back."

Kelle stepped in. "Better for now if we draw them away from you and the people of the Meadow. Can you hide from them?"

The Mayor of the Meadows and the Captain of the Rangers looked at the young corbie as it danced. The Ranger, after a few seconds, spoke, "They came quickly, which means they have no army at their backs. That sort of magic requires power to spare just to move seven and their steeds. Anyone who falls into the path of The Seven will die horribly, but they are just seven, no more. They cannot search the endless forests of the Meadows for us, and they will find no succor, provender, or even a half-tallow to light their wet, cold, bedside. And their horses are not immortal."

Kelle clapped the warrior on the back. "Then, we will flee, dragging these evil knights away, if you will hide and succor the former prisoners as if they were your own kith."

"We will. Time is short—who will guide you to safety? Virdea is not to be traveled lightly, and even the Yellow King's Road has hazards."

"I will!" It was an impish young man in parti-color leggings and a performer's frock. He was tall, maybe 180 centimeters, with a mobile face, a knowing, almost jester-like smile, and oddly enough, shy eyes that said to Kelle he was not as comfortable as he was trying to be. "I am the Troubadour, Douglas of Bourne, poet, performer, and ready to follow my queen anywhere!"

"I am no queen. We do need a guide," Kelle said.

The man brushed his curly hair out of the way. He was unarmed and seemed to be of two minds. His legs and arms acted like the world was his own stage, and each move they made was a laconic attempt to communicate some hidden joke to a loving audience. His shoulders and the muscles of his face, though, showed an almost boy-like alarm at what the rest of his body chose to do. He seemed to speak as a way of bridging the gap in his inner dualism. Kelle looked at the Mayor and the Captain of Rangers, who both shrugged.

The Troubadour said, "I am a stranger to these men."

Kelle asked, "Where are you from?"

The Troubadour replied, "I travel this road gathering stories."

"And you wish to tell ours?" Kelle saw much to like in the handsome Troubadour. And they needed a guide.

He looked thoughtfully at Kelle. "Yours I think is being told. You, however, are a rod placed on a building to protect it from a storm. It may save the building, but you attract lightning. And I have great respect for people who ride storms and live to tell the story."

Kelle felt a purple thought at the back of her head that said, <*I like him.*> She turned and looked at the Chevy. "You're hired, Troubadour."

THE PRETERNATURAL CLOCK

In 1955, Chevy designers were planning for the upcoming 1957 model year when a request from the highest ranks was passed down that the new vehicle should include an electric drive clock. Unlike most elements in a car's design, whose size and mass could be changed based on the needs of the engineers, the space allotted to the clock was set even before the dashboard design was started. It would be 3-1/2 inches wide and 1-1/2 inches tall. No more, no less.

There is a small group of clock lovers for whom this clock has always been a mystery of design. Researchers have never found a design order for the clock. The other Chevy dash instruments all have a long and storied history of development. The clock popped into existence seemingly from thin air. The second oddity was its accuracy. Watches, even expensive ones, slowly creep away from true and need to be reset. Owners of the Chevy noted that their car clock seemed inaccurate and some bought replacements. It was only in the presence of hyper-accurate timepieces that it was recognized that the Chevy clock was actually more accurate than nearly any other source around it.

And it was only in 2017 that a clock designer for the government, playing with an old Chevy 1957 model electric timepiece, wired one into a sounding rocket as part of a Rube Goldberg project. The clock would trigger a series of events that would include, at the end of the process, firing a large parachute to allow an instrument package to be retrieved.

It is a little-known fact that GPS satellites have a timing subroutine in their computers that adjusts the time shown on the satellite's clock with that of one sitting on Earth. This is a real-world and observable effect of time dilation that arises from Einstein's good old $E=MC^2$ formula. Objects moving at different apparent speeds also experience time at different apparent intervals. A second is not a constant, but a variable defined by velocity.

The main issue with all of this is that science has never defined what the resting state of the universe is. That is a fancy way of saying we can tell how fast we are going compared to some other object, but not against a fixed point in space that is not moving. That point in space is a conjecture of theory. It is as if our universe has no zero on its number scale of velocity.

When the '57 Chevy clock was retrieved from the recovered sounding rocket after two years in space, it was keeping perfect time as if time dilation did not affect it. Someone, in 1955, had designed a clock that was immune to the speed of light time errors and arranged for it to be installed in many of the 1957 models of American passenger sedans. Soon after this was discovered, it was also discovered that most of the thousand or so remaining original clocks disappeared.

These facts have absolutely nothing to do with our story.

Or do they?

CAT DANCING

DATE: FEBRUARY 2, 2018
LOCATION: PETERBOROUGH, NEW HAMPSHIRE

The universe is not a simple place. It is full of twisty conundrums that astound and make a simple human pause to genuflect at the greatness of creation. Right now, I was looking at the little-known area of math and science called reality physics. That part of physics defined what we know as reality. One of its core proofs was created by Dr. Kelle Brainerd, a very young savant who was the product of a decidedly third-rate university education at the University of South Florida. Her formula was the proof that gave us the globular world and thirteenth-dimensional space concepts.

$$(\pi\hat{\ }13) / df(subx\hat{\ }4) = UC$$

Another way of stating that formula is that the universe is made of dimensions, with each dimensional concept requiring a new dimension to hold it. A point is a one-dimensional construct that needs a second dimension, or you cannot set the point. And things run swimmingly for twelve dimensions. That turns out to be the last dimension you actually need, but since that old rule exists, the universe expresses in a thirteenth and unsettling dimension where math breaks down and mathematicians hide in terror.

A stable and unchanging universe would be happy with eight dimensions. Then, you would have lots of happy quarks doing quark-like things in swimming harmony, and humans would exist in a slightly rounded space where it is possible to throw a disk off a cliff and have that disk strike you in the back. Math is so well ordered here that spheres can be super-packed more densely than any other dimensional construct (well, except twenty-four-dimensional space, which is a bit silly any way you count it).

Now, a lot of the math-challenged will argue for a tenth-dimensional-space-construct. In fact, I bet most of the readers have by now said, "How can you fit more than six dimensions into a Calabi-Yau manifold?" having themselves run the most basic calculations through a basic dimensional calculator. Dr. Brainerd was thinking the same thing when she was reading about data artifacts that appear when you use a statistical tool called Spherical Mexican Hat Wavelets process to analyze pictures taken in space. That is one of the data systems used to discover the supposed Kardmen Gateways, weak spots between universes and thus between the tenth-dimensional substrate. It turned out that the appearance of a second universe intruding on ours disappeared when you simply used another statistical model. Sort of like Bayesian Lumps that occur in Tester's T that make weird people seem to win presidential elections once in a while. To quote Dr. Brainerd's fifteenth hypothesis, "Shit happens, and then you quark."

It was when considering the Mexican Hat that Dr. Brainerd decided to test tenth-dimensional math against string theory. Strangely enough, when she recalculated a series of basic proofs but substituted an eleventh-dimensional-universe model, everything worked out just fine. And in twelve dimensions the worlds purred along on graph paper and the cherry soda she preferred. It was, as I hinted, the thirteenth dimension where the universe became unstable and her computer showed her a blue screen of death. In fact, she could only make some of the assumptions work by changing an important variable to the square root of negative one and then came to a point where her calculation required her to double that figure. Her MathPro application would never again run the same afterward.

Dr. Kelle Brainerd existed. She was born in 1994 and, in front of me, were her second and third dissertations, both written before she was twenty-three. She was not successful at publishing articles and seemed to be unable to land a faculty position anywhere. I had called one of the universities she worked at and spoke with two people on a hiring committee that had rejected her.

"You ever hear about the theory of the third candidate?" one of the professors asked me under the rose.

"No, what is that?"

She laughed on the other end of the phone. "No professor wants to compete against another professor who can do differential equations in their head. If we wanted that, we would have applied for work in the industry or in private think tanks. The dean does not want student complaints from having a professor that is smart either. This is an age of acting dumb or being dumb, even in the university. She was the best candidate from a research standpoint. The gentleman that came in second was a great teacher. We choose the guy who had a great accent, was six-foot-three, and could bake. The third candidate is who you hire."

Dr. Brainerd was the type of person who could propel her department, with the right colleagues and support of a good chair and dean to the stratosphere. Most people in the modern age just wanted someone to teach the poorly designed and universally hated Freshman Seminar without trying to change it, make waves, or really, do anything. These popular professors would be easy pickings at tenure time, but even this protected the status quo. With no backbench, the players who dress out for every game become very important.

There was a cough at the door of my office. I looked up to see Rochelle Standish holding a package from Amazon in her hand. Rochelle was thirty, hawkish, and thin, with wire-framed glasses and hair that expressed her mood. Today, it was done in a tight bun that I felt sure was applying pressure to the top of her brain, making her angry at me and the world.

Political expediency had created the title of Administrative Assistant for Rochelle. In reality, she was my brilliant research fixer. Common of people her age and temperament, she had attended the University of New Hampshire and tripled majored in political science, anthropology, and environmental science. She had followed it up with a few years at Antioch New England studying environmental communication. With a finely honed mind, a wide and liberal education, and college debts in the hundreds of thousands, she soon found out that it was nearly impossible to earn a living at anything she had studied. She worked as a camp counselor making minimum wage. She wanted to teach anthropology or political science in high schools, but those jobs had gone the way of hadrosaurs into some murky tar pit of human existence. She could teach disinterested students at cut-rate community colleges who had long ago given up trying to offer the same classes as senior colleges did and now were content with handing out buckets of college credit, but when only thirty percent of her first class passed the first test she was fired and replaced with someone who would give out a lot of "A" grades.

I met her when she was serving tea at the Toadstool Bookstore. She was not a good tea maker, but I saw her reading a book by David Brin, and I knew she was not ordinary, so I offered her a job on the spot.

She turned out to be surly, unpleasant, mad at the low pay I offered, continuously furious at what I asked her to do, and ever ready to tell me off in "Marvin the Paranoid Android" fashion. Brain the size of a planet. She was always ready to unionize, forever banging doors closed or giving me the silent treatment for a week or more on end. Under her breath, she called me "his ass-holiness."

She was also brilliant. Requested research projects came in less time than I thought was possible, written neatly in little folders, annotated with information that went way past the request, organized into tabs, and often included pictures. Travel arrangements were always clever and never relied on the routes that the different transportation modes insisted on their passengers taking. Sometimes she found a limo service that could complete a hop faster and cheaper than an airline. She loved to put me on trains that had me sleeping eight hours without needing a hotel. I was forever being surprised with a seat on a small corporate plane, helping pay the fuel price of a flight they were taking anyway.

Her memory for details was amazing, and her education assured me that I was getting an immense brain dump on nearly any subject I was interested in. Her only negative, aside from being hard to deal with personally, was her complete and utter disdain for commas. I bought her a copy of Grammarian Pro, and that went away.

She walked into my office holding the Amazon box and stopped short of my wall covered with pictures, articles, and lines of twine. Since her normal delivery method for reports to me was to fling them through my door, I doubt she had seen the inside of my workspace this entire month. She tossed the box on my desk and said, “Jesus.”

She was wearing her standard, thermal tights, a huge blue sweater, and big tan boots. When she wanted to tell me the office was cold, she would add big earmuffs and a wool jacket. “Should I call the FBI?”

I set the dissertation down in the pile reserved for Dr. Kelle Brainerd’s work. “No, she has been missing for a few months as far as I can tell, but she was not kidnapped.”

There was an icy silence between us. Then, she stepped around my desk and ripped open the drawer that I hid my spare Valproate. Finding the bottle intact, she walked over to a filing cabinet where I kept a collection of bottles. She rifled through the glass bottles and came up with the bottle of Bénédictine Single Cask, turned, and held it out to me like an accusation. "You have been drinking this?"

"Some."

She threw it back in the filing cabinet. "Asshole." She turned and left my office in high dudgeon.

After she left, I took my small knife from my pocket and opened the Amazon box. Inside were two books. The package had a gift card that said, "J. L. Sullivan's Irish Pub, February 6th, noon."

I ducked my head around the corner into Rochelle's office. "Find out where J. L. Sullivan's Irish Pub is."

A minute later she said, "Lancaster, about three hours north."

"Put it on my calendar, noon, February 6th. Mark me out all day."

"Why not?"

Roads in New Hampshire had a habit of starting and ending places where you did not want to be. This meant the traveler had to be a bit stealthy about finding a way to any given destination. It was almost like the towns in the state were coy, and detecting the direct approach of a traveler, they would slide over a few valleys to assure the main road passed just a few dozen miles away from them. Lancaster and Peterborough were proof of this concept. A topographic map of the state suggested that a road like 202, which snaked its way through Peterborough, should be a north-to-south artery that gave access to the mountain region that included Lancaster. Instead, State Route 202 delivered on its promised route for about thirty miles, to the town of Henniker, and then went scaring off across to the East like a magnet drawn to metal landing on Concord.

I had very close to no desire to hump this way and that across the state on the Federal Freeways that followed only the most obvious river valleys, so I took 202 to 114 and then followed a series of twisting backwoods roads north that generally followed Highways 3 and 4 with a few odd New Hampshire switchbacks. This was the real White Mountains so not a great drive in winter, as the roads never truly get plowed but instead become narrow paths with heaps of snow crushed up on the verges of the traffic ways. As you drive, you alternate between following slowly behind an old sedan ill-equipped for the winter weather and being nudged on your rear bumper by a kid in a fifty-thousand-dollar SUV and parental-paid insurance. Despite this, the drive is relaxing. I have a car kit, and at times, I wish my car would just skid off the road and leave me stranded for a week in the snow to eat survival rations and build a survival shelter.

Lancaster is a weather-beaten little mill town propped on a fast-flowing river that represented the community's main reason for existence. In the age before chemically powered industry, mills powered the American economy, and those mills depended largely on the energy potential of falling water. Those days are over, and towns like Lancaster would be the perfect spots for a person to settle down, raise a family, and live the rest of their life, except they have not figured out how to attract reliable employers to their communities. The towns are too conservative to really develop a tourism base, and way too conservative to make the infrastructure improvements that would attract the intellectual pioneers who would love to leave Boston in the dust and settle in the great white north. Despite this, Lancaster survives. And it has a pub.

The pub was a well-run, small bistro designed to mimic an Irish bar but without copying one exactly. Dishes made with pulled pork and Jack Daniels muscled out the few Irish specialties on the menu. I sat down at a table and ordered Blarney Stones, corned beef and sauerkraut that was fried like a German sandwich rather than Irish provender. A homemade Guinness sauce was a genius concoction that had never seen the shores of The Emerald Isle.

They were out of Bénédictine.

I was just diving into a main course and wondering if the sum of my experience in the North country would be a tasty meal at an obscure pub when a man sat down across from me. He had a long face, a half-smile, and curly blond hair that reminded me of a precocious boy. He was wearing a warm sweater and creased slacks, and he still had his mittens on, although his coat must have been discarded at the door. He removed the hand gear and held out his hand. "Nelson McKeeby?"

I shook his hand over the table. "Can I order you something?"

"I ordered from home."

They brought him fried pickles, a vegetarian burger, and a side of baked beans that the waitress claimed was made "without pork." For a few minutes, hunger consumed him. I picked at my chicken, more interested in the gentleman across from me. He politely, but with gusto, devoured his meal. After he had reached the halfway mark, though, he stopped and smiled at me. "You haven't asked me what this is about."

"No, I have not," I replied, channeling Errol Morris.

He had a subdued, almost self-conscious laugh. "Do you remember the reading you gave at the Keene Toadstool?"

"On biomythic hypernarrative?"

"I was there," he said. "And I read the books you were flogging."

"You and three other people," I said. Then I considered it. "I make most of my money from nonsense sex guides and absurd sugar baby advice books. I do not remember you."

He laughed again. "You do not remember me because I was hanging about the children's section, behind where you were speaking. You said some profound things, or so I thought."

I looked at my drink. "I was probably drunk."

"No, quite lucid." He pulled out a small notebook and quoted from it, "Line up a group of Chimps and a group of Men. Write down what makes a creature better than the other and then test each group. In the end, you have defined your own bias and not the fitness of either species to survive."

I nodded. It was from my paper on autism. "Do you have an autistic child?"

"Me?" Another laugh, gentle and self-conscious. "No, it was the first thing you said that made me take notice of you. It was the second that made me invite you here. You said, 'If your main characters disappear into a tornado, you have no other choice but to follow them through, or the story is not complete.'"

I said, "That is me also, you should be commended on your ability to take accurate notes."

"Thank you, but what I am better at is reading things written upside down. I passed by the desk you were sitting at and saw you had a pamphlet called, Bashful, Kansas."

I nodded once again.

"You are studying Virdea."

For a second, I was caught flat-footed. Of course, I was writing a story about the land of Virdea. I was also, in a strange way, part of a conspiracy to aid four creatures in their trek of self-discovery across the land of Virdea. I had made no secrets of this to anyone, but I had not advertised my work either... To have a stranger pick up on it...

"It is called synchronicity. How is it that I am in the Toadstool to see a speaker that attracted exactly three people speak on a subject that is definitely not about Virdea, yet somehow come up with that answer? The answer is magic, or thirteenth-dimensional matrix algebra, or Wittgenstein's ideas of picture theory coming back to haunt us like a curve ball thrown into a hurricane force wind. Bashful does not exist, and thus, it never existed, but find a picture of the town in a library in Kansas, and suddenly, are you so sure it is fictional?"

His words were so tuned to my own thinking it seemed like they were coming from some omnipotent being in my head.

> (Fourth Person Note: I have been silent these few pages reading the narrative as avidly as you, the audience, has, so do not write some thesis accusing Mr. Eric Pallado of

being my alter ego in this tome. It
is untrue and actionable.)

"I know the people existed, until they did not. I know they exist, someplace else."

"Virdea" was the one-worded response.

"Correct. I wish it was named Oz. It seems like a good children's fictional story."

"Children's stories are very rarely fictional. Children do not think that way. They have very literal and linear ways of considering the world, and if you lie to them, they always know." Eric's words were punctuated by knowing smiles and small pauses for laughter.

I said, "Tell that to Santa Claus."

"I will if I ever get back to Virdea," he replied.

Silence hung between us. I sincerely believed this guy; my credulity having grown these past months with each new discovery. Certainly, the raven part of my brain was pecking at the human side, demanding I dance the dance of joy despite weighing seventy-kilograms more than would make this safe. Cautiously I said, "What is your relationship with Virdea?" I took out my notepad and showed it to him, and he nodded assent.

"For almost a decade, I was the cat tender of Mount Washington." He said that with such an air of pride that I thought he expected me to know what that meant, but he quickly followed it up. "There is a set of oral histories taken from what is supposedly a dubious source in the New Hampshire historical society that have a European preacher, John Elliot, questioning a Native American shaman of great magical ability, Papisse Conewa, which means Child-of-the-Bear, about his beliefs and telling the shaman of his own Christianity. Reverend Elliot was surprised to find out that Child-of-the-Bear could speak a very rough version of Latin, almost guttural Italian, and when asked where he learned the language, he was told that the 'Gods of the Great Mountain' taught him the tongue. It turned out that the Abenaki tribe, of which Child-of-the-Bear belonged, believed that the top of what we call today Mount Washington was a place where the gods could travel to our world, and we could travel to theirs.

"You have to realize that the term 'gods' in the Abenaki languages is more easily comprehended if you understand that they actually have three sets of gods. Two sets, the beings of the ancient age and the beings of the golden age, are very much like Western gods. They create the world, make the sun rise, and cause the spring to come and the stars to twinkle. A few of them are heroic in nature, but they usually serve the great gods.

"Then, you have the gods of the present age. These gods are not so much deities but beings with interesting and different powers. Some earned their powers by traveling to a strange land after scaling to the heights of a great peak or surviving a storm at sea in a tiny boat. Some originate in the golden lands and climb down from the great peak to spend the rest of their existence doing extraordinary things among humans. Some are not heroes but just baneful creatures who escaped from this alternate land that must be dealt with by humans with trickery and cunning.

"So Papisse Conewa takes Elliot to the top of the great mountain where they resist a great storm, and he then meets a cat with 'prodigious fur and big paws' who seems intelligent. In the worst of the wind, they follow the cat step by difficult effort, and suddenly are standing in a calm vista on the edge of a great plain of rivers and cities, which Elliot claimed, 'Stretched for leagues before me.' They then follow the cat again and are beset by great winds, which forced them to shelter in a small rock crevice or be blown from the top of the mountain."

I sip my Coke and ask, "And I can find this story where?"

"Right in the archives. The original was stolen, but last I checked there was a mimeograph of the original."

I wrote hurriedly. This was hardly paid data, but it was interesting. I wrote down "the golden land" and "gods of the present age." Then, I drew a line between them and wrote "Virdea." "Well, thanks for the information."

Another self-deprecating laugh. "I am sorry. There is more if you like."

"Really?"

"In 1820, a pair of farmers climbed Mount Washington on the newly cut Crawford Trail, looking for accessible stands of timber. They were working while there was enough snow on the peak to allow them to move the timber down by sledding. In a crevice, they found the frozen remains of a man dressed in chainmail type armor and armed with a curving sword. They call him the Viking Man and claim that he has been frozen on the mountain for a thousand years, despite the fact that Washington does not have year-round snow. The body and armor was stored in Berlin, New Hampshire until it was purchased by one of a group of men and women who were financing construction on Mount

Washington. Only the femur of the body and a dozen links of chain were retained in a lead storage crate."

I wrote down, "Strange man in armor. Impossible to be Viking preserved in snow." To Mr. Pallado I said, "This is great."

Eric nodded, smile still on his face. "Twenty years ago, I was hired by the group that runs a tourist agency called the Commune. I was to pose as a weather taker on the mountain, but my job was twofold. The first of my jobs was to tend to the cats that live on the mountain. You only see one or two, but there are about twenty. Most come and go during the storms and otherwise stay out of sight. Those cats are like cats anywhere in the rural lands that live with humans, they have a job. A farm cat hunts mice and rats. A town cat entertains their tense human masters. A cat on Mount Washington guides travelers to and from the land of Virdea."

I nodded like a dumb idiot. No matter how deep into the rabbit hole I climbed, there was always deeper to go. "Virdea you say?"

"I am not sure the math around it, but if you have a certain gift, a way to see the world, you can use a place where there are high winds to get to Virdea. Or perhaps, as a weather person myself, it is more accurate to say that magical gates between our reality and the alternate universe of Virdea cause unusual windstorms due to pressure imbalances between the worlds. It works like a battery in some ways. Electrons move along a wire from one pole, and they are replaced by electronics moving along another wire to a second pole. In between, work can get done. In this case, the work is to shove a bunch of air around."

"So anyone can get to Virdea on Mount Washington?"

"Heavens no. Heck, that orange-face baboon of a President would have ICE camping out all over the mountain and be demanding we build a wall around Kansas, Iowa, and California. The right people in the right place with the right skill sets can get to Virdea. Or sometimes, it's just dumb luck. Magic works that way. Look, last year, first week of October, this guy was messing around at the summit, drunk as a lord, and he claimed he was at a party in 2048. He falls through a windy passage, wakes up in a land of aliens, and gets told they will return him to his own time. Back through the gate, only the poor sap lands in 2017 maybe 300 kilometers northwest of Cheyenne, Wyoming, and immediately asks to see the president of the town. Where and when he is from, towns are incorporated like companies to get tax breaks and better treatment in the legal system, but not in Cheyenne in 2017. Guy gets locked up until the state hospital people come and get him. Only he never makes it to the hospital and has never been seen since."

"That's amazing."

"I have never been to Virdea, but one thing Virdea does is act as a highway. People from one time travel there, have an adventure, and then find their ways home again. Sometimes though, home is not where they want to go, so they never go home. They use Virdea to land themselves in a time and place where they can have their happily ever after."

"Can I meet any of these people?"

Eric started scribbling on a piece of paper. I took it. "They have a commune in Massachusetts. Ask for Regulus." He then thought a second more. "You should know this. I cannot tell you how I know, but look up this person."

The second slop of paper said, "Mamma LeDeoux, New Orleans, around 1820. Look for references to her husband, José Gaspar." I held the slip up and said, "What is this?"

"The car."

"What car?"

"The 1957 Chevy. It is the name of the soul that inhabited it."

I held the paper tightly and thought of the Lady Violèt from my dreams.

THE SAGA OF THE JOURNEY OF LIGHT

DATE: 10TH DAY OF THE BEAR, 3684
LOCATION: THE WINDING STAIRS, GREAT MEADOWS, VIRDEA

Deep in the recesses of a yellow-orange main-sequence ball of hydrogen, superheated by its own mass pressing down onto a dense center, 600 million metric tons of hydrogen are fused into the element helium each second, generating enough energy to launch a purple 1957 Chevy at the speed of light nearly 770 billion times, should you happen to have a rail launcher capable of that feat and a pair of jumper cables made from 117 million tons of copper. For our story though, we do not have to launch a 1957 Chevy of any color, we just have to scoop off a little bit of that energy, not even enough to raise the outer edge of a gnat's wing a single degree for a single second, to generate a single photon.

We want to understand that photon, but it requires the ability to do thirteenth-dimension math to really comprehend it, which in this story only Dr. Kelle Brainerd has. Instead of understanding, we have to simply describe its journey using parlor tricks and inexact English. To understand a photon, our mind wants to stop and describe it, but by stopping it, we have caused it to cease being a photon. It turns into heat. Instead, we have to describe its journey through the parlor game of English exposition, telling a story where the photon is spoken about as being on a journey, the proof of its existence only occurring when it ceases to be a photon.

That photon starts its journey by being flung out from the star at an immense speed but in a straight line. The first noodle bender that the reader must understand is that photons never deviate their paths as they fly through space. It is the shape of the universe that makes it appear to us, in our ignorance, that it has deviated course. Stand in a clear pool of water and look down at your legs. If you are positioned right, your legs will appear to change direction. It is a mistake to see the light as the culprit. It simply kept going straight. It is your legs that exist in a bent dimension.

The next noodle bender is that light defines the shape of the universe. If it was not for that pesky cat guarding that photon of light, we could sit down with it, pour it some tea, and ask it what shape the universe is. And it would sip its tea and say, a "triskaidecagon," probably thinking us the smallest sort of moron, since the mathematical reduction of a triskaidecagon is a perfect sphere, and we often see these around so we should have figured it out for ourselves. However, since the tensors involved in those equations are much harder than the sixth-grade knowledge of math most of us has, the photon would be wrong to think worse of us. Which is why it has the most boring job of the universe, to fly straight.

Anyhow, that jolt of light flies forth from the sun has a speed of C (which is a great way of avoiding using up numbers in your type-box since C means the speed of light in any situation, which is 299,792,458 meters per second in a vacuum. Buying more nines when you run out of them is a pain in the ass, so you want to conserve and just use C).

Just as an aside. 299,792,458/(13^13) is supposedly a really important number, at least according to Dr. Brainerd, but this chapter is already convoluted enough and probably at risk of being edited out of the book entirely, so let's just return to the main topic.

Eight minutes is how long our speck of light travels from the sun until it runs into something—the world upon which Virdea sits. Here, it runs into a particular part of the world, a small bit of steel mined in Pennsylvania (on a completely different world, Earth) and forged into the barrel of a pistol. The barrel is attached to a Smith and Wesson Model 3 revolver, and that is a story to tell. It was purchased by Richard Guys, a mule skinner, in Kansas City, Missouri who then lost the weapon to Sergeant Abner York in Fort Hayes, Kansas, who coming upon financial troubles (caused no doubt by his gambling), sold it to Thomas Ward Custer. And from there, it is obvious to the reader who currently owns this device. You see, it was this very pistol that Captain Custer jammed into the chest of a fifteen-year-old boy and attempted to snap shoot the youth. It was empty, the hammer falling on a cartridge case that had already been expended. The pistol had traveled a long distance from that small grassy knob in Montana Territory on June 25, 1876. It was now the iconographic weapon of the Lakota warrior Rains-a-Lot, sometimes known as Jim Smith, lately a Troubleshooter for the Dustin-Rhodes Corporation.

There is a philosophical issue that may bother the reader about this very pistol. Since the weapon changed hands, it had fired around 29,000 cartridges, an amazing feat that had required over the years for each part of the pistol to have been replaced more than once. Thus, no single part that was included in the weapon in 1876 is still in place. Yet, its owner and most other people consider it the same device, a continuity of form if not of parts.

Leaving aside the potentials that progressive mortality offers, the current issue at hand is the precise geolocation of the pistol. The bit of light that started in a star eight minutes ago bounces off the pistol and travels with many other bits into the eyes of the earlier mentioned Dr. Kelle Brainerd. Once there, it strikes a series of organelles and is converted into electricity, which flows into a variegated membrane that communicates its contents between thirty-seven and fifty-nine times per second to the grey matter of Kelle's visual cortex, a little nubbin of brain matter at the back of the cerebrum, passing through the traffic cop of the lateral geniculate nucleus. Once at the visual cortex, it is copied electrically and flashed throughout the brain to allow it to trigger memory, mental responses, and the like. In the case of Kelle, it has triggered her to yell in a dominant, powerful voice. She yells because the pistol is being held by her friend and ally Rains-a-Lot against the head of a young man with red hair and a scarred ear, wearing a snappy trader's outfit and finely brogue-patterned shoes.

A writing instructor of mine, years ago, told me that it was always best to start in the middle of the action instead of having a long buildup. Technically, I agree, but frequently finding ourselves in the middle of a scene without explanation can be confusing. So allow me to rewind the videotape of reality a bit and start at the beginning. Reality is cheap, so sadly all we get in rewind is static and a zip squeal, but at least the tape moves fast through the annoying barrier of duration.

Rains-a-Lot felt the mud beneath his toes as he ran. He was a passenger in his own life, the world a winding kaleidoscope of forms and images, a hurdy-gurdy playing a personal soundtrack that only he could hear. The people of the meadows were fleeing north under the protection of the Rangers, but The Seven were an existential threat. They carried death as sharpened metal and had a willingness to use it.

It was Ivy who had tailored this plan. The Rangers and the Meadow folk were speaking about a final fanatical resistance to honor their savior when Rains-a-Lot's partner had become intensely angry. The people of the Meadows would not expend themselves in saving the travelers from Earth. He would instead form the sole rear guard.

Rains-a-Lot had heard the Gallic fatalism in his partner's voice as a promised self-destruction to pay a karmic debt that no one should owe. The Lakota had listened to his partner and only friend plant the seeds of *Götterd*ämmerung with him wearing the costume of Siegfried as if he were the Yellow Hair. He had seen *Der Ring des Nibelungen* in Chicago in 1888, and in his own nightmares, it was now the theme music for Little Bighorn, although he never assigned Custer a role greater than a character from a satyr play. It was the young soldier who cried in thirst that was more heroic to Rains-a-Lot, or maybe his friend Grass-Waving who died in the first charge, whose shade watched him in his terrible deed.

Whatever the reason, he had finished listening to Ivy plan his own elaborate death scene and to the agitated ravens screaming a defiant staccato of complaint, so he waited a few seconds, then Billy Browned his partner. Standing over his unconscious form, he said to the Troubadour and Dr. Brainerd, "Follow the road down to the plains, I will meet you at The Lonesome Gate."

Dr. Brainerd looked down at the unconscious Ivy. "You hit him."

Rains-a-Lot nodded. Anglos tended to say the obvious when trying to make up their minds. The Troubadour asked, "Friend, why should we trust you when you just did that?"

"I am Rainmaker."

There was silence. The Troubadour said, "Dr. Brainerd, we must go, how fast can your automobile carry us?"

Rains-a-Lot had already closed the conversation. The Rangers were moving the civilian army to safety. One approached. "Are you really the Rainmaker?" The Lakota looked at him in the eyes. In Virdea, people developed reputations, becoming legends, just like the land of Rains-a-Lot's birth. You knew the names of Spotted Owl, Lame Horse, and Angry Bear. You knew the Long Hair, Devil Chivington, Tall Chief, and Red

Cloud. Meeting them was not required when you could meet their reputations. If you did cross paths with them, you knew who they were, and in a land where reputations were tested and tested again, you could be sure that the actual creature holding the name was either whom they said, or soon to be lost to their own legend.

And Virdea was where legends were as real as the plains. Rains-a-Lot had seen the process and built his own legend, but he had never had himself tested. To tell the truth, he was afraid. He had failed a test before, failed and watched as an unimaginable price was paid. Even thinking of the price, of the cold day when cannons and Gatling guns had rained down hell on frozen and starving refugees, caught his voice in his throat and turned his thoughts and being inward.

Rains-a-Lot returned the French semiautomatic rifle to its storage box in the trunk of the automobile and took the older folding stock paratrooper model that fired with a bolt-action. He took two boxes of ammunition for himself, and the silenced Whitney Wolverine, which he gave to Kelle. He looked at the Troubadour and said, "Betray her, and I will hunt you."

The Troubadour said, "Peace friend, I am straight up."

Rains-a-Lot nodded and said, "Ivy will be awake soon. Drive slow." He then left.

Running silently is a skill that requires athleticism, dexterity, and acrobatics. Rains-a-Lot had stripped to the waist, showing his eagle tattoo acquired on the docks in San Francisco. He saw from the corners of his eyes the ravens that followed him. They were like guide stars, trail blazes, and information posts. They led him to an overlook where he saw The Seven riding in single file about six-hundred yards away.

Each wore fifty pounds or more of armor and rode horses barded in fifty pounds more. Despite this, they had urged their mounts to a trot. It was reckless, but the warriors were so close to the travelers; they could be on them in a half-hour.

The Lakota pulled the rifle from his shoulder and locked the aluminum stock into place with a click. He opened the action and stripped five rounds from a stripper into its magazine, then closed the bolt, chambering a round. The weapon went to his shoulder, and he pulled his bandana down onto his left eye. Releasing his breath, he pulled the trigger.

The nine-gram bullet left the shortened muzzle of the French rifle at around 800 meters per second, spinning on its axis because of the rifling of the barrel. The travel time from the barrel to the target was just shy of 650 milliseconds. Despite the high speed of the bullet, five-hundred yards was a long way. When it had reached its target, it was moving at 640 meters per second, had drifted four centimeters to the left of the aim-point, and had dropped 148.5 centimeters, corrected mostly by the sights, which had caused the shooter to raise his barrel. The bullet missed human targets but struck Mussiǔdragu's horse in the rear flank, causing it to throw the owner and charge out of control.

Rains-a-Lot stood and yelled in the common tongue of Virdea, "I challenge you, Seven; I am Rainmaker the Silent. I challenge you in the ballad of death!" He fired another shot with no visible effect, turned, and ran.

How do you measure the love of another man? It was here in his mind Rains-a-Lot imagined Ivy laying out stripper clips in front of him, pulling the rifle's tiny bayonet from its concealed holder and fixing it, then shooting himself dry before being trampled by the great beast horses. You measure the love of another man by refusing their offer of a useless lonely death. Instead, you snatch his futile attempt at balance from his teeth and turn it into something else. You turn it into a test of legends.

The rain had started to fall as the ravens yelled fearsome insults into the darkening sky. Rains-a-Lot ran. He knew where he ran. It was a minute, maybe less, before the horses' hooves crushed him. Ahead he saw his target, a deep marl trace, maybe seventy yards wide and two-hundred yards across, in some places submerged by water. Several dry paths showed where animals had crossed the slimy expanse. The grass closest to the slick was taller than the rest of the field, maybe because heavier animals could not eat it without bogging down.

Clutching the rifle to his chest, he slid into the slick and came to rest nearly covered in seeping marl. He then used his cover to move, kicking his legs like a frog, to a point where water and mud covered him completely. He only allowed his eyes and nose above the filth, channeling a crocodile on the hunt. His submerged ears heard the world as if they were plugged with cotton.

Rains-a-Lot could see it in his mind's eye. To the horsemen, it was magic. One moment, their prey was in front of them and vulnerable, his small victory about to be paid back in death and blood. Any good prey turns and runs, but what prey disappears into the ground? They charge him down nonetheless, unaware that the grassy field was a mud bog. Their charge is horrible, slower by half than Rains-a-Lot could ride a plains pony in his youth, but like some unstoppable force spit forth from some White hell. Then the war horses, 18 hands and a solid ton of meat, stumble into muddy gumbo and come to a sudden halt, turning end for end and throwing rider and barding like chaff from the grain.

Except for Mussiùdragu, who had already lost his horse and was walking purposefully toward Rains-a-Lot's hiding place. Like any good magic trick played by a trader to impress the children of a tribe, if you kept back and watched carefully, the trick was easily revealed. The armored six, riding at full tilt, had fallen for their prey's careful subterfuge. The dismounted seventh could see exactly where Rains-a-Lot had wound up.

Looking over his shoulder, Rains-a-Lot could tell the first six were bogged down, and without their squires and pages, it would be an hour or more getting clear and collecting their horses, assuming they survived the headlong charge. Mussiùdragu, though, had ripped his great helmet from his head, his huge smile causing his black handlebar mustache to lift into the air like absurd crow's wings.

The Pain Worm said, "Peasant or hero, thing of the mud. Who do I defeat today?"

It was the nature of magic and Oz. Great characters did not fight silently. They prided themselves in their incantations, benedictions, and tedious riffing boasts. You fought a name, and both sides acknowledged it so that historians could get their stories straight. It was custom.

It was also idiocy. "The muddy one must be a peasant."

"The muddy one is Rainmaker."

Rains-a-Lot nodded and slung his rifle over his shoulder. He looked up into the sky and saw Raven. Maybe it was only a single raven, but he liked to think that Raven could protect him, even here.

"Would you like to hear my death poem?"

"Only if it can be said before I reach you."

Rains-a-Lot pulled his Bowie knife, starting to sing softly as the Pain Worm picked his way across the soft ground.

Ma la be da mun
De la mum da wum.

The knight was an "invincible" warrior. As was mentioned, he was cocooned in fifty pounds of steel forged by the greatest armorers of the day. His sword, called Dragon's Bane, was a giant Zweihänder with its lower portion left unsharpened, allowing terrible thrusts as well as immense, eviscerating swings. The man was an expert at controlling the weapon, able to inflict immense pain or immediate death, like a surgeon with a finely made scalpel. He was also a great hero, and that meant something, at least in Oz.

De la mum de dumb
Be la mum the mum

"Your song is hardly fit for a warrior; I hope it has an ending."

Rains-a-Lot replied, "This is our last dance!" and leapt.

Mussiǔdragu was preparing for a rainbow swing, an attack that could cut an individual in half. It was in keeping with his personality to go for the flashy, but dangerous, attack. It was dangerous because a very well-trained armsman, lightly armed and armored, could rapidly move inside the blade's danger zone. Faced with such a charge, the correct response would have been to shorten the blade, present the shoulder, and use a spear-like two-handed thrust. In such a case Rains-a-Lot would have had a difficult time avoiding the terrible piercing attack, lacking armor, or, once he made contact, the ability to maneuver. Mussiǔdragu did backpedal but planned to continue his swing. His failure was in footing. It may seem hard to believe, but the burly knight dressed in armor while executing a fast backpedal heel-to-toe and a mighty rainbow swing from the waist exerted nearly 25 psi of ground pressure, almost as much as a passenger car, and such a car would have sunk half-afoot into the marl just by engaging its reverse gear.

Rains-a-Lot dove, using all his mass to push the knight off balance, catching his sword with his left hand when Mussiǔdragu's swing was aborted by falling, and riding the man down to the ground. His right hand shoved his knife up under the arm, where the warrior's tournament armor lacked the normal chain chest guard of true plate and mail worn by less-well-paid knights. Both warriors knew what it meant as the blade severed Mussiǔdragu's aorta, causing him to feel like a water bladder being upended within his chest.

"How does your death song end?"

Rains-a-Lot stared at the dying eyes of the Pain Worm. He did not answer the question; he had never had to sing his death song to its very end to discover this.

The noise of the bogged down warriors came to his attention with a flood. Most had abandoned their horses and were trying to wrestle their way from the deeper marl to where it could sustain their mass.

Rains-a-Lot watched the men flailing around in the mud, beating their injured and, sometimes, dying horses, whose screams were chilling into the inner marrow of any person who had grown up with the majestic animals, for whom manhood and a living horse were connected in a deep, religious way. Living so many years in a culture for whom horses were falling to the side, replaced by mechanical beasts, even when some of those beasts were obviously intelligent in their own ways, had made Rains-a-Lot feel the lost part of himself the horse represented.

Warriors, Rains-a-Lot thought, *live so much in the past.* During the between times, you ponder meaning in a way that was often quite disturbing. Seeing the dying horses, he thought of the dead at Wounded Knee. The old man who had guided him there had wept at the frozen bodies, hands stretched to the sky, flesh torn by cannon, and rattling automatic gun named for a man Rains-a-Lot would never say. The horses, no matter how fierce and deadly, were the innocents.

With a sad heart, he brought the Saint-Étienne rifle to his shoulder and shot three of the horses with obviously life-ending injuries. He knew it was futile, but he shot each of the struggling men as well, stopping to push a clip of five rounds into the weapon's open action, discarding the little aluminum strip that held the bullets onto the muddy ground. He emptied the weapon again, then loaded a new stripper clip of bullets, feeling a thrill at how easily the weapon accepted the new death-dealing cartridges, at the horrible genius of humankind. He could not blame white men alone for this because he had watched his brother load a tube of bullets into a spencer he had stolen, firing and firing with a laugh in his heart at the blue coats whose rifle fired only one.

And Rains-a-Lot had stood in the cold, frozen morning and gazed on the dead of the Lakota, and the fact they had no horses, those had been taken from them, and the fact that they had been shot from every direction, like the dancers in a circle suddenly turning inward and shooting the dance leader in the middle. Unlike that cold winter day when the magic of the Ghost Dance failed, as the old man predicted would happen if Rains-a-Lot was not present to bless the dance, his own shots had no visible effect on the knights. They were heroes, and the magic of the world of Virdea protected them from a wanton death while, unfairly, did little to protect horses—animals that Rains-a-Lot felt deserved more protection.

He fired another shot and yelled in the lowland tongue, *"Sugnu u Rainmaker* è *mi dispune à qualchissia ch*ì *vulete ammazz*à *a mo fam*iglia, *affruntate* è *mute!"* It was a challenge of men, to tell each one of the so-called heroes that their quest led only to his tent and their doom at his hands. These men might not fear as he did, but they would understand that riding their horses down on his friends as though they were poor, doomed peasants, robbed of their magic and fleeing their homes in terror, would not be possible. He had no word for love in his heart, not anymore, but he had the vengeance of his body to bring down on anyone that would trample his brothers and sisters. Old Man had named him the warrior with two hearts, his own, and that of the warrior whose heart he had eaten. *So be it,* he had thought.

Rains-a-Lot turned and left. Six armored men with three horses, even if they abandoned their kith's body to crows, could not possibly follow his friends at pace. They would follow but would need to arrange for logistics to come from a friendlier land. They needed squires and armsman, scouts and spies. He had gained them a week, maybe. Maybe much more.

Rains-a-Lot turned onto the Yellow King's Road and started to track his friends. The Chevy was easy to track. It rutted the ground and made a clear impression from its 7.50-14 tires. The Chevy was the only large mechanical device to have ever traveled to Virdea, give-or-take the alarming story of the USS *Eldridge*. He took several attempts at obscuring the track, but he realized it was impossible.

Two other tracks were associated closely with the Chevy. All that meant was that within a day or so, someone else had passed this same point. The first track was a pair of panje wagons, led by two larger and two smaller people. Animal dung showed that this group was driving reindeer, a common animal in the upper Meadows. The shoes of the four people became signatures after a bit. It was easy in a place and time when shoes were handmade. For example, the smaller people wore moccasins that had not been differentiated for left or right foot. They were large, floppy, peasant's booties. One of the larger people wore unusual fey slippers, while the largest person had forester's derbies. In one place, he kneeled down and gave Rains-a-Lot a perfect impression of a fancy brogue pattern. These were traders, carting goods down from the Meadows, and unlikely to have had anything to do with the recent battle. They were not traveling fast, and after a half-day Rains-a-Lot came to the place where the Chevy passed them. They had pulled their carts over.

It was the three people who followed that concerned Rains-a-Lot. They moved slowly as well, but faster than the traders. Their track came and went from the road, as if they were scared to travel on it except where the contour of the land demanded it. They smoked cigars, cheap lowland-made Corbies, sometimes called "Weeds" for their unpleasant odor. They also wore lowland sandals.

At one point, they left the road. He followed them off and saw they were using sharp-edged weapons, maybe short swords, to cut succulents from the undergrowth. Rains-a-Lot tasted the bulbous plants they were eating. They were juicy, full of water, but lent a horrible bitter taste. Whoever ate these was starving.

He was moving almost twice as fast as the Chevy and even faster than the traders and their panje wagons. He soon reached a point where the three men-in-sandals met the traders in the panje. Their tracks all left the road.

Rains-a-Lot felt the unease of ending magic, the time, and place of finality. He saw Raven sitting in the tree above him, head cocked, knowing what the next page read as if it had been written by him. Fear, existential and bold, filled the Lakota's heart, fear for what he would see and never unsee, fear for what would be left un-praised.

With silent stealth, he took the rifle from his shoulder and unscrewed the bayonet, drawing out the thin, deadly thing. The smell of lubricating-oil brushed the edge of his senses, but beyond that he could smell finality in the form of human death. With care, he pressed the bayonet into its tube and heard it lock closed, such a tiny human sound but more than he wanted to make. Rains-a-Lot then took a stripper of bullets and placed them between his teeth, before finally, slowly, working the bolt action of the rifle, inserting a cartridge. The weapon had no safety other than the training and understanding of its user. Rains-a-Lot never carried weapons with mechanical safety devices. His safety was his finger, and the brains below his skull.

The three men in soldier's sandals had spread out and were creeping through the glades almost on their stomachs, as a snake might stalk a prairie dog. This was maybe a day past, but the tale was still written on the canvas of the world for any to read.

Rains-a-Lot thought of himself as two people. The first part of him was a child of many parents who ran free among the dark-haired, humor-filled men of his tribe while he was also raised by the fierce, ethical, and kind Blue Flower and her husband. This man was conflicted, scared, and sought friends to protect him from the terrors of the world, but his voice was silent lest he commit the unpardonable sin of crying in front of those he loved. The second part of him was darkness, silence, and precise action. That Rains-a-Lot was like his Cherokee father's accounting books, he merely was a vessel to catalog information in precise rows before acting dispassionately on the balance. He was a stone.

It was 1944 when Rains-a-Lot murdered seven men, leaving two alive. He had arrived the year before, bewildered and hollow, and had taken a job as a bank guard when he was hired by Col. Bernard D. Bernstein to act as a civilian guard for two art historians, Paul S. Dustin and Amanda J. Rhodes. Fit, strong-backed men were hard to find, and it was assumed that bank guards were honest, knew how to use a gun, and did what they were told. The ten-person group had been organized by the Department of Treasury, of which Bernstein was a member, to determine if certain gold objects were art, or if they were simply unusual-shaped bullion capable of being melted down into more traditional bullion shapes. For weeks, sitting in cold tents, eating bad food, and occasionally being bombed and shot at not only by Germans but by friendly forces, Rains-a-Lot listened as the seven other trusted servants planned to kill Dr. Dustin and Dr. Rhodes and escape to Brazil on a Brazilian Navy transport bribed for the purpose. Later, when it was all over, he listened as Dr. Dustin told of being tied up and abused, and how suddenly from nowhere the silent Lakota who had said nothing to his knowledge since being hired, had pulled an unauthorized silver revolver and executed the turncoats, although they had modern military weapons.

What Rhodes could not understand was that Rains-a-Lot did not really kill those men. He had not killed Thomas Custer. He had not killed two men at Drexel Mission. It was the other part of him who had done it, the warrior-hero that knew no fear, who could not lose faith, and that did not allow his mind and soul to wander the hill-studded grasslands of his youth looking for buffalo that had long since died. And it was not he who looked at the bodies of four poor traders hanging from the Eucalyptus trees of a small camp. Rains-a-Lot sat silently for a minute, waiting to see whether the bandits were still there, waiting to ambush the rescue party, but he thought not. Finally, he took the spare ammunition from between his teeth and returned it to his pocket, ejected the round from the chamber of the rifle then dropped the remaining rounds from its magazine, reloaded the weapon, and closed the bolt on an empty chamber. He then folded the stock to its side and slung it from his back.

The ground told the story. The men in sandals ran in upon the camp, and there were places where people rolled on the ground while someone stood over them. Then each trader, three men and a woman, was stripped, tied up, and hoisted by the ankles. The three soldiers then stood and talked for a while. One had put on a new set of shoes, the brogues he had seen earlier. It was likely the soldiers were interrogating the traders to discover where their cache of money was. A small broken chest showed they had found it.

He looked clinically at the hanging traders. A large man with ringlets in his dark hair, muscular with dark skin, and a kind face, even frozen in death, was likely the trader. He had fought, his hands said at the end he had fought with no weapon, and maybe he had marked his prey. The woman next to him was older, grey-haired, and strong-muscled. Her skin was copper, as if she came up from the delta and was likely a trader herself. Next to them were two boys, pale skin with shocking blond hair.

The wagons were torn apart, but the reindeer, maybe two sets of seven considering the size of what they hauled, were gone. Defeated soldiers turned highway agents when fleeing their lost battles.

There was a noise behind him.

Rains-a-Lot drew his revolver and turned, but the noise was not ambush. It was the blond youth on the far right coughing blood. He was cut so many times, deformed in such a terrible way, that he had appeared to be dead.

The Lakota holstered his pistol and drew his Bowie. Bringing the youth down gently was difficult; he had to swing him up and hold his across his shoulders while he parted the knife then throw the knife down as he caught the mass of the young man. On the ground, the child opened his eyes and said things in strange tongues.

Rains-a-Lot needed water. He found a cockade that had once proudly covered the head of one of the traders, a beautiful thing now cast into the dirt, and ran down to the clear flowing springs that must have been the reason for this little campsite's location. Into the hat, he scooped as much water as it could hold, then returned.

He was fifteen, and like the elder two traders, he had fought before being trussed up and tortured. Rains-a-Lot cleared the child's mouth, finding a piece of ear like a wad of chewing tobacco behind his lip. The child had, in a final act of defiance, bitten the ear off the man who was hoisting him into the air. With a catch in his voice, Rains-a-Lot said, "I call you, Ear-Biter." He gave the water to the child, then cleaned the wounds, especially where his stomach had been cut open and his entrails exposed. Rains-a-Lot then reached into what he called his medicine pouch: a small belt pouch concealed under his leather jacket that contained what medical supplies he had.

Rains-a-Lot jabbed the child with two doses of morphine, which caused him to relax and look back with stunned eyes. Then, he closed the wounds, disinfected them, and used clothing strewn about the ground to give them what bandaging he could.

There was no time to bury the dead, and he did not know what words they would have said over them. Rains-a-Lot doubted any god he knew would be able to see here, but he tried to do what he could to respect them. He cut the three remaining traders down, lined them up, and covered them in fallen leaves.

The child weighed hardly anything. Swaddled in bloody rags and limp from morphine, he could have been a game animal, cleaned and being returned to camp, but most humans did not treat game animals as he had been treated. Rains-a-Lot slung the rifle on his front, fashioned a carry-all to strap across his forehead, and took up the youth across his shoulders and back. The carry-all was needed, as Rains-a-Lot intended to run.

There was no real way to tell how old Rains-a-Lot was. In his own mind, he felt as if he were in his thirties but was probably a decade older at least. There is a timeless nature to Oz that changes how someone born on Earth sees age. Still, a run of twenty miles that would have been easy in his youth was now gut-busting, especially carrying as he guessed was a hundred pounds of dying child. The Yellow King Road was the main artery of commerce from the Great Meadows, through the city-states of the plains to the delta lands, but here in the highlands, it was hardly more than a path and passed civilized holdings only occasionally. It was five miles before Rains-a-Lot even saw another sign of human habitation, an abandoned travel lodge. Ten miles past that he located a trail that was well-traveled and followed it five miles into the rugged hills that marked the edge of the Meadows before coming to a cluster of meager wooden shacks, two of which had great clouds of steam coming from them. By the smell, it was a village of sappers, people who collected and refined various forms of resin and sap for medicinal and chemical uses.

The central structure of the cluster had reindeer antlers over it, meaning the public house, and a man in a grey and red robe tended piles of drying herbs, his jaunty, floppy soft cap showing his occupation as an Herb-Key. Rains-a-Lot saw the man as educated and not dangerous, at least not immediately, but likely a person of some authority. He leapt onto the wooden porch that surrounded the building and laid the child down onto a table, sweeping it free from bundles of plants.

The man screamed in one of the upland tongues. Rains-a-Lot knew only the words of the city-states and no more. He did have trade sign, which was not that different from the sign languages used in his youth. He gathered up the man by his robes and pointed his to the child, and then signed, "Protect."

Deeply bearded, dark-skinned, muscular men poured out from the public house. Some of them had two-stick tension bows, cumbersome dart throwers that were cocked by holding one stick and pushing another away, after which a small bolt was held in place on a third length of wood. They were cumbersome, but also deadly. Most also had bronze knives shaped like thick leaves, able to feed their user, or in a pinch, be used as a deadly tool of war. The men all yelled, until a final being stepped from the building.

She was tall, lithe, with golden hair and long limbs. Her eyebrows were slanted above almond shaped eyes, and her voluminous hair was swept back at the sides to reveal pointed ears, larger than a humans and ethereal in their fragile appearance. She looked about and waved her hand gently, then looked at Rains-a-Lot and said in perfectly accented Lakota, "You are the Rainmaker."

Rains-a-Lot felt he had no choice but to respond. "I am he."

She looked at the warrior for a minute then in a soft tone said, "Have you met one of the Fey, an Olda Shihe?"

"Only in tales and dreams," he replied.

"Did you violate this child?" was the next question.

"I rescued him. His masters were murdered by defeated soldiers fleeing the Battle of Lark's Field, only he survived of four. He seems to be from the outer ways, a drover," Rains-a-Lot explained.

"His name?" the Fey asked.

Rains-a-Lot considered this. "I name him Ear-Biter."

The Fey tilted her head and acknowledged the name. "You are of the Conspiracy of the Ravens; I have heard them speak from the trees."

"I am not. I am from Dustin-Rhodes Company protecting a young woman of science." He looked about him and found a place to make the child more comfortable.

The Fey clicked her tongue. "I did not ask whether you were from the Conspiracy of the Ravens; I state this as a fact known to me which you are not permitted to argue. You are the Travelers the trees speak of, and you must return. Killing the Pain Worm is only the first of the tasks you are assigned by fate and by the gods."

"The child..." Rains-a-Lot started to ask.

The Fey spat, "Is neither kith nor kin. Now go."

Rains-a-Lot drew his Bowie knife. The Fey and the sappers stepped back and grew tense. The weapon was fine enough to be magical, but it was not; they looked at it with hunger. Iron and steel were made in the low-lands, but this weapon was made from a steel far better than could be manufactured by anything but magic in the lands of Oz. Rains-a-Lot took the blade, made a cut with it on the back of his left hand, and said in Lakota, "This blade is payment for the family who takes in this child. And with it my oath as a warrior of the Lakota, the Rainmaker, to forever render aid."

The Fey stepped forward again. "Impressive warrior. You have too much death in you, but you speak from the heart."

"I have too much failure in me. This must not be a failure, nor must I fail in my commission to protect Doctor Brainerd, which calls me now," he said.

"Ahh, the good Doctor. Consort with wizards and you will find them hard to be shut of. The Conspiracy of the Ravens is to bring you into the presence of the Queen of Fire and Ice in the Green City. The Doctor will not be safe until you do this and more. The story cannot be complete until you do so." The Fey turned and spoke with the sappers, and one man, burly, with a single eye and curled black hair stepped forward. He held out his hand. Rains-a-Lot handed the knife over and bowed. The child was then taken away.

Rains-a-Lot felt the compulsion to speak fade. He nodded at the Fey and turned away.

Then, he ran. He ran slowly, so he could track. Where once reindeer pulled two carts, they now were driven, some with pack-loads, by three men. Two of the men wore sandals, and the third wore the trader's fine brogues. And soon they started to travel with the 1957 Chevy, and for two days moved as a group, camping every twenty miles or so.

When Rains-a-Lot found he could run no more, he fell into a fitful sleep. The Old Man would come and visit him here—he had offered him mastery over the Ghost Dance if only Rains-a-Lot would come rescue his people at Pine Bluff. And he tried. Yet, the old man had given him mastery over the Ghost Dance, at least in part.

On the third, the Yellow King's Road entered a place known as the Winding Stairs. The Chevy and the reindeers slowed down as they left the Meadows for this series of tight switchbacks that would finally see the end of the uplands, traded instead for the endless steppes of the city-states. Here Rains-a-Lot gained rapidly, cutting the switchbacks and moving with dangerous haste. He had already decided to seek the legendary Vangar Outfall, the great vantage over the steppes that also was one-hundred-forty feet above the supposedly magical Vale of Tears and the Fell Lake. Here, a single jump could cut twenty miles from his travel.

Rains-a-Lot arrived at the Vangar where a sluggish meadow river leapt out from a precipice into space and stopped to look out at the world displayed before. The lands of Oz from this vantage looked like a painting of the world inked onto some canvas. Tiny images of hills, trees, brown steppe grass and red-painted buttes, competed with stripes of green and blue flowing rivers, and onto this, the gods had spilled all of the animals that roamed the lands. Humans were so tiny when you looked at their works from here. He stripped completely and wrapped his gear tightly in his clothing. He then threw the gear over the cliff. It landed in the water below and seemed to be okay. There was no need for a wind up. Rains-a-Lot closed his eyes and composed himself. This was another thing and no more. Things were nothing but a hill in a sea of grass, to be ridden over or around. He opened his eyes and dove out into space.

He fell for only a short time, less than four seconds, but in that time his velocity increased to nearly forty meters per second. If he had leapt onto concrete, he would have landed with nearly 47,000 newton meters of force. If Rains-a-Lot had not entered the water in a streamlined form, he would have been smashed to pieces by that force. Instead, he entered the water in the way he saw birds hunting fish, like a dart. Unlike Olympians, he had no desire for beauty. He entered the water feet first and made no effort to stop himself as the darkness of the water engulfed him.

When he again had dressed, he went to where the Yellow King's Road passed the beautiful lake. The Chevy was less than a day ahead from here by its tracks.

That night he caught sight of the car. It was parked in front of the first public hostel he had seen on the road. Around the car was picketed dozens of reindeer, several horses, and a sizable number of carts and wagons. Out front stood Ivy, obviously looking out for his partner. Music and the chatter of a crowd emanated from the public hostel, which was more like a beach shelter than a closed-up building.

"Rains-a-Lot!" he yelled and ran forward, hugging the Lakota. Rains-a-Lot permitted it. There was something deeply Gallic about hugging, and Ivy would, at times, revert to a character of himself, weeping, sputtering in French, and praising some saint for his good luck. It had to end quickly though. Ivy stepped back from the embrace and said, "What is wrong?"

The small photon of light mentioned at the start of the story is generated in the sun and moves on its way to Oz.

Rains-a-Lot went to the herd of reindeer. They were picketed in clusters by the owner. One cluster had the exact number. He invaded the herd space, causing a racket and bracing the lead deer. The pack lead was not in a mood for being manhandled by a stranger, but Rains-a-Lot did not care. He grabbed it by the head, wrenched it under his arms then reached for his front hoof. Ivy stood and watched. When Rains-a-Lot released the deer, Ivy followed him into the public house.

The hostel was not a dark dive. Except for the direction of the kitchen and the sleeping space, it was open by way of a series of large windows. The windows had thick wooden covers, but these were swung down in the temperate weather. A large cupola provided further light. Inside this caused the room to take on a dapple as shadows and beams of light crossed each other, blocked and let through by the movement of dancers and the swaying of trees.

The music was an odd elution of two stringed instruments and a drum, plus at least one woodwind. The result was an odd elution of sound as two different, syncopated melodies competed for attention of the crowd. Occasionally, the beat and the tempo would dissolve into concordance, but this would only last a short while before exploding forth again into competing tracts.

The crowd was either involved with heavy drinking or dancing on the floor. The dance itself was disjointed as the dancers elected to follow one of the two music lines or tried to find the middle distillate resonance between them. Rains-a-Lot stopped and scanned the crowd.

The Troubadour came up to Ivy and Rains-a-Lot and said, "Dr. Brainerd has hired three guards to guide us to the Green City."

Rains-a-Lot looked back at Ivy, who shrugged. Then, he saw Dr. Brainerd. He took off through the crowd, expecting it to part for him or be run down, followed by Ivy and the Troubadour.

Kelle was dancing with abandon with three young men. All were from the steppes with bronze skin and curled hair, two of them gold and brown, and the third with red hair. The red-haired man wore a trader's *szabla* and fancily brogued shoes; the lower lobe of his left ear had recently been lost. Kelle saw

Rains-a-Lot and smiled a huge smile, ran, and jumped into his arms. The Lakota held her stiffly, then set her aside. She turned to Ivy and said, "Is he okay?" Ivy did not respond.

Kelle turned just as Rains-a-Lot drew his silver revolver, grabbed the red-haired man by the neck, and pressed the revolver to his temple.

"Rains-a-Lot!" Kelle yelled.

One of the other soldiers tried to draw his *szabla* but found he was staring down the barrel of Ivy's Browning. "My friend here has an issue with your friend." Rains-a-Lot jerked the red-haired man around and made sure he could cover all three soldiers. "Correction, he seems to have a problem with all of you."

"I do not know the cretin," came a reply.

"Ivy, what is he doing?" Kelle asked. She was being restrained by the Troubadour.

The crowd formed a circle around them. Traders solving personal issues was one of the main forms of entertainment these hostels boasted.

Rains-a-Lot kicked the man's shoes. Ivy said, "My partner wants to know where you found such fine footwear?"

The man cringed. "I bought them. They were purchased." Rains-a-Lot clouted him.

One of the men in the crowd said, "They look like the fancy ones Heartly Simes wears."

"I do not know any Heartly Simes!"

Rains-a-Lot kicked the soldier's feet from under him and planted him backside-up on a desk. Ivy said, "Does anyone know Simes's markings for deer?"

"I do." It was the same man. He left the hostel and returned. "It is the same brand."

Rains-a-Lot made a sign to Ivy.

"He wants rope," Ivy said.

Another trader said, "Five fathoms right here."

It was handed to Rains-a-Lot, who tied the man's feet then threw the line over a beam in the cupola. The crowd then hauled on the line until he hung from the air. The other two were disarmed and treated the same. Kelle stepped up and said to the red-haired man, "You seemed like a civil person, tell them what they want to know."

Rains-a-Lot pulled a hat, crushed and abused, from his jacket. It was a cockade. The crowd recognized the hat as well. One of the traders, a jovial man in normal times, approached and said, "I think you have proven your point." He took the hat and said, "Take your friends and go. Traders look after their own."

Rains-a-Lot stalked from the room, followed by the others. He noticed Kelle pausing to look back at the soldiers.

TAR PIT BLUES

DATE: JUNE 16, 2018
LOCATION: BEVERLY HILLS, CALIFORNIA

The cab dropped me off at the Quaking Fear offices on Wilshire Boulevard, a 25-kilometer-long parking lot that started off as a trading route for American Indians. I had been to the Brazilian consulate several times in the past decade, so I had my ride drop me off at South Hamilton by the John Wayne Statue across from the Saban. Quaking Fear and the Brazilian consulate were new Hollywood architecture, while the Saban was the older, cooler stucco of the city of lights. It was a hot morning already and would be a hotter day. The shade around John Wayne's equestrian statue was worth standing in, preparing for the risky proposition of a dash across the traffic at Wilshire.

As I stood in the relative cool of the statue, I saw an eccentric man across the street. He was dressed in a British business suit and a bowler but had some sort of special effect machine going that made it look like his body was made from oily smoke instead of flesh. He stood there, staring at me, at least it seemed so despite his lack of eyes, and then tipped is bowler toward me. I nodded politely.

The dash across Wilshire was, as I thought, a dangerous sprint as drivers, stacked up through the light and turning right and left, were eager to kill pedestrians.

This was a mixture of work and obsession. Most of my money nowadays came from either strange little books I wrote for the self-publishing trade, or creative consulting on scripts and websites. In my blue Porta Brace director's bag was a script review that Quaking Fear's creative manager Stephen Scales had requested. Creative managers like Stephen were the little muscles that made everything in the entertainment industry happen. In a city where thousands of people had a line on a friend who knew a guy that bowled with someone that had a script, Stephen was the guy who actually could get all of the major creative players in the city into the same room to fund, plan, write, sell, and market a creative piece. Every bit of television you see, every second of film that rolls past your eyes, has somewhere deep in the core of its being, a Stephen Scales cranking the handle.

In that ecosphere, I was a useful parasite. At one time, I had been a go-to director and producer for rapidly produced television programming, but that was another life. Now, I was a creative consultant. People hired me because I could help them figure out effective and producible ways out of creative dilemmas.

Effective and producible is the key. A writer produces a script with a guy having a nightmare about another person having a nightmare during a recursive drug episode. Someone with money options the script. Then, everyone sits down to figure out how to make that screwed-up Masters of Fine Arts project into a real, shootable, producible, and marketable product.

At some point, the group of experts will admit they need one more person, and that is me, the pinch hitter who untwists plots, fills in story holes, and hammers out details of historical or technical relevance, while eliminating with extreme prejudice the scenes that will cost millions to shoot or that will risk the lives of A-list actors. My name never shows up on IMDb because, in the larger scheme of things, I am not the most important person in the room.

Stephen had sent me a script set in the Great War, which the author described as a French *Saving Private Ryan* with an American main character. He did not say anything about what he wanted, which meant he just wanted a read to knock down implausible things.

I walked across the street and entered the building in which Quaking Fear had its suites. Security was always tough on these buildings, tougher in fact than the Brazilian consulate, which in my experience could be invaded by three cub scouts dressed in stormtrooper outfits. The guard on the front of Quaking Fear's building was a Mexican American wearing a precisely pressed white uniform shirt and dark slacks, an ID badge clipped to his shirt pocket. He had a serious demeanor and a determination to do his best to protect his charges from the random distractions of tourists, nut cases, and job seekers that on any given day descended on the doorways of the entertainment industry. He looked at my face, at my picture ID, checked the roster of invited guests, then gave me my pass.

The intern at the receptionist desk for Quaking Fear was a serious-looking young man with a serious-looking Flock-of-Seagulls haircut and a string tie that shot down the entire "serious" effect. Before he could do his job, Stephen Scales came out to meet me in the lobby. "Nice to have you in person, Nelson."

"Am I late?" I asked.

"No, just in time," he replied.

Stephen is a little under 180 centimeters tall and dresses Hollywood casual in a dark blue button-up, jeans, and sneakers. He keeps his unruly, brown curly hair under careful control and has a standard hipster beard, although his humorous baritone voice is anything but falsely hip. His only sign of Hollywood pride is a pair of clear-framed glasses.

"Nice glasses," I said.

"You like them?" He walked me into their conference room where a dark-haired woman and an ill-dressed pauper sat.

"I liked the thick black ones also," I said.

"Times change you know." He turned and said, "This is Estelle Wiggands, marketing, and Pram Bout, the scriptwriter. Everyone, this is our creative consultant on *The Yanks are Coming*, Nelson McKeeby."

I nodded and put my things on the table. An older man came in and set a coffee service on the table. He did not introduce himself, but if the owner of the company wants to deal with refreshments, that was his gig. The whole group tended to be that way, it was how they stayed in business against bigger shops. Since the service arrived close to me, I looked at Estelle and then at the pots of hot water and coffee. Estelle said, "Red tea." She was dressed in this wonderful wrap-around in chocolate brown that made her seem like some great Ashanti princess. She took the tea like royalty and said, "Thank you." Then, she put enormous reading glasses on her face that had optics that were so thick they almost popped from their frames. From her stack of papers, she took an accounting sheet.

I looked at Mr. Bout, and he said, "Coffee" with a fidget. He was dressed in a tweed suit coat, a white shirt with a pattern of palm trees, a Sinhalese flag pin with its rampant lion holding a sword clipped neatly to his lapel, and stained jeans held up by a thick black leather belt. He had a notepad in front of him where he had drawn stings of little figures that looked like mice with curling tails alternating with curly cues. I passed him his coffee, which he took with thanks, spilling a little on his script.

Stephen shook his head when offered a drink, so I took a red tea of my own and sat down. Mr. Bout opened the conversation by saying, "Mr. Scales, I thank you for this meeting, but I am less than understanding its reason."

Stephen smiled. He had a good way with nervous creatives. "We brought in a creative consultant as the first step in getting your script produced. He gets no screen credit and makes no actual edits to your work, that is up to you, but he does talk to the three of us about everything from tiny details in your writing up to big issues we might not be expecting. Do you agree, Nelson?"

Stephen was so much better than I was at this. "Yes. You went to college to write, correct?"

He said, "Yes, Iowa."

"Great college. And you learned how to make a great story. Your script is read by a dozen people who help you mold the characters, get the exposition just right, and you figured out how to get the characters from page one to page done without ripping a hole in the universe," I said.

He looked at me a little bewildered. I continued, "Now, someone likes your script. And then, you find out you are just part of a large team that will be bringing this story in for a landing. One of the hardest parts of this is that your script will be going through a vetting process. People like me will poke holes in the story that will distract certain segments of the audience from the big picture. Other people will be figuring out if your script is producible in terms of time and money ... and who will watch it and where it will be watched. Then, the producer and director will get your script and they will do all sorts of heinous things to it. Finally, an actor who knows more about playing effective characters to an audience through a film camera than every one of us combined will have a 'go' at each line in real-time, and then an editor, and that original producer will drop your favorite scene because in the end, it just did not work well enough to be included, but it will end up on the director's cut."

The poor guy had no idea. This author was a first-timer, although this was probably why Stephen had a team to talk to him. He looked like I had just beaten him with a sandbag. "What if I do not want this," he asked in a low voice.

Stephen laughed in a way that was calculated to put the poor guy at ease. "Then you should have written a novel about a fantasy world!" I looked over at Stephen, and he shrugged. He had been monitoring my progress with my last novel and had provided a lot of support, but it was still funny to think about in some ways. I wondered if someone would ever write the story of me writing the story of the land of Virdea, then I tabled that as metafictional nonsense.

"I am here to provide suggestions," I said.

Stephen slapped the table. "Go ahead, give him some of your ideas."

I took the script. "Your story revolved around a tough American from the streets of the Bowery in 1914. He hears about the war coming to France, so jumps on a ship and arrives in time to join the French army, arriving on the battlefield riding a cab and helping save Paris. "

"That is the first part," he said.

I replied, "August 3, your street fighter is in New York as war is declared. Average cheap berth ticket is ten days, unless he has a LOT of money. So he shows up in Brest on the 13th, assuming he read the first edition to carry the war news and spent eight-hundred days of pay to get his ticket. To get through induction when every regimental station is throwing arms and uniforms on soldiers was sixty days. None of that was training. A lot of American volunteers coming from the states, and there were some, would not be accepted into uniform before 1915, usually over legal concerns and the simple reason that there were still too many French."

Mr. Bout was a little defensive. "Suspension of disbelief—"

"—Is great when you have this poor guy charging across no-man's-land to pick up an officer and carry him back to safety. You only have so much of that stuff, why not save it for when you need it?" I asked.

"So what do I do?" he replied.

"There are only two sorts of Americans in Paris who made it into the frontlines quickly. The first was upper class Americans in the expatriate community who had friends in high places. A lot of these guys ended up enlisted in the army of their adopted nation. The other was entertainers. This is where your Bowery tough comes in. He could be a boxer, respected by a group of soldiers for how tough he is, he wins them money. They are called up and in the rush of the first days of the war he says, what the heck, and joins also."

I was not sure if Mr. Bout was ever happy, but after that, he seemed less combative and made sheet after sheet of notes on his yellow writing pad. By the time Ms. Wiggands and I started putting some prices on the trickier effects scenes, the scriptwriter almost seemed to be relaxed. When the meeting broke up, Stephen ducked close to me. "I am busy all day, but I have a driver for you, and this."

He handed me a paper. It said, "Mark Zales." I looked back at him.

"He works with Randolph Homey. The boss arranged for a meeting with this guy up in Glendale at five o'clock. The driver can take you to dinner afterward, drop you off at your lodging, or you can catch a flight out, whatever works."

"Thanks, Stephen."

Stephen hesitated. "Everyone in this industry gets obsessed about one project you know. The project that will never sell. That thing they believe will be the one they will be remembered for."

I nodded.

"Just don't lose sight of the fact you have a lot more stories in you. What happened to that hospital story, you know, from the patient's perspective?" he asked.

I shrugged. "There may not be time to tell it."

He clapped my back. "Dude that is defeatist thinking. Anyway, we will catch up soon."

I walked down past the receptionist and past security, returning my badge, and took a turn into the parking garage. Waiting for me was a petite, thin young woman in a paisley sundress. She was definitely a child of the sun, with long, straight blonde hair, a diver's tan that said she spent a lot of time in scuba gear, and only simple jewelry, a turquoise ring and an Asian-style beaded bracelets. She had the proper "spunky" attitude for young adults striking out in the entertainment industry, a smiling "can do" feeling that was tinged with a normal amount of self-protection and deferential respect for an unknown charge. I walked up to the company Tesla and said, "Are you my driver?"

The woman smiled softly and said, "Sallie." Once we were in the car, she said, "Where to?"

"Someplace to eat lunch, then we have a meeting in Glendale at five o'clock."

She nodded and pulled the car out of the underground lot and onto the side street leading to Wilshire. Her unspoken destination turned out to be the Tar Pits. Driving with LA confidence, she cut off onto 6th and snagged us street parking just east of Levitated Mass by the amphitheater. We walked down to The Counter for hamburgers and soft drinks. Food in hand, we returned to the pits to sit by a pair of sad mammoths, one slipping into the tar.

"It is like a screwed-up form of time travel," I said.

Sallie seemed transfixed by the mammoths. She turned and asked, "How so?"

"A mammoth slips into the tar, and thousands of years later, it comes out the other side. What is screwed up is that they end up preserved, but dead? It is the conundrum of Disney's head."

I have never been any good at reading facial expressions unless I use parlor tricks. The young woman assigned to me today as my minder stared across the pond and did not reveal what she was thinking. Her shoulders though had hunched when I mentioned Disney. "Disney wanted immortality, so he had his head frozen under the theory that eventually, they will thaw him out, pop his head on some new body, crank a few electrodes, and Disney will wake back up."

Sallie said, "You don't believe in that?"

"Not really. It may happen someday that magical head regeneration is invented, but I think intelligence is dynamic. If you do not have a place to store it, then it goes away. Frozen heads might retain the ability to process intelligence, but the actual thoughts that make you unique? I just doubt that it is that easy."

Sallie turned to me. "When I was in college, I had a tough time. I was from this conservative place where you could know the truth simply by watching one television channel and asking one person for it. Then, I went to college, and they made me a scientist, and I realized I had lost something in the process."

She was fidgeting with her bracelets between bites of her burger, some organic and probably meatless monstrosity. "Is that where you are today?"

Sallie smiled. "No. I have no idea what I want to do with life, but I am past some of that worry. You see, I learned about pteropods."

I blinked at her.

"In 1804, a scientist named George Cuvier described these tiny, calcium-shelled creatures that are all over the ocean. Now, here is what is so cool about these critters. They live their lives, die, and rain down from the ocean sky to form beds of calcium. If the oceans have more acid, their shells get smaller. If it has less acid, then the shells are thicker." She smiled at me. "You do not get it."

"Not really," I said.

"These tiny little things are part of what regulates the acidity of the entire ocean. Take them away, and the ocean would swing wildly from acid to base and back, and maybe the entire thing runs off the rails when one of those swings does not come back again. However, they are time travelers too. They do not live through time travel, but instead, they communicate across time. We can look at the shells of these creatures and tell something about what the world looked like on a very big scale," she said to me.

I nodded. "So communication is time travel."

"Any scientist knows that." She took a drink of her soda. "You are the guy writing the Virdea book."

"Yes," I replied.

"You are telling people the book is nonfiction?" she asked.

"I think it is real," I replied.

"You know what I think? Creativity is the calcium shells that protect society from the acid that builds up around us. You are like a little snail crawling across the face of human existence, telling your story, and your shell is getting eaten away, but in the process, you are telling these people in the future, people who will never know you personally or understand what it took to write a story, something about the world that exists today. Who cares if anyone believes you?" she said.

We were back on the road. Wilshire to Highland, then the 101 past the Hollywood sign, and then climb into the hills on Barham. Traffic was hard on Ventura, so we took a side road called Zoo Drive that punted us across the pathetic Los Angeles River via Riverside Drive, then onto Sonora through Little Armenia to the Brand Library. We find parking and walk past the yucca-defended green cross that sadly asked us to save our trees in a state with no water, constant fires, and little desire to stave off the onrush of desert. Sallie and I walked up to the Japanese Tea House where a man with a huge smile stood.

"Who is this?" He nodded at Sallie.

"She works for the people who set up this meeting," I replied.

The man seemed to think this over. He was dressed in a button-down shirt, sandals, and jeans, and oddly enough, had a single wooden drumstick in his hand. "Thanks for your help, miss."

I shook hands with my guide, and she went back to the car and drove away. It was not until she was out of sight that the man said, "My name is Mark. Do you understand the limits of this meeting?"

I turned back to him. "You can get me a meeting with Randolph Homey."

"Nope. Someone I know thinks you have something serious going on that might be worth Randolph

Homey's time, and someone I know agrees with that assessment. I cannot get you a meeting with Randolph; I can only pass information to him if I think you are not complete bat shit." He turned to the teahouse and said, "Let's get tea."

The tea service was outstanding and traditional. It was the type of ritualistic event that kept everyone silent. When I could speak, I said, "I am a researcher."

"Word I hear is a creative consultant," he said.

I nodded. "Sort of the same thing. People hire me to make their stories plausible. To dig them out of plot problems without going too far out of bounds."

"Where were you during the last season of *Lost?*"

"I did not get that contract," I replied.

Mark said, "So people actually pay you for this?"

"Sometimes. When they need to figure things out fast," I answered.

"So where does Randolph come into this?" he asked.

I drank some tea from the little cup in front of me. It was getting cold. "He is an interesting convergence of creativity. Did you know he was asked to write a song; then he goes home, writes it, comes back, and it is one of the greatest songs of all time?"

He blinked at me. "I was aware of something like that. To tell you the truth, I do not talk to him much about his musical past, except as a fellow musician, you understand."

"What he did seems impossible," I said.

"That would be an odd statement considering he did it," the man replied.

I looked at the red lacquer of a lattice that spread out behind Mark. It was ornate and beautiful, a classical piece of Japanese handcraft. So much pride went into such a utilitarian object. After a minute Mark Spoke again, "Not everyone follows the same path into music, you know."

The tea service was likewise, beautiful. It was light blue and eggshell, with darker blue highlights and a hint of silver. Each piece was functional yet alluring. Mark kept speaking. "A lot of musicians follow different paths into the art. They buy instruments and practice in garages; they hang about the scene learning from older players. And they figure out the deck is really stacked against them. Even more so today. The music industry has been teetering on two wheels since the payola scandals, helped along by the likes of Phil Spector. Somehow though, music gets made, and people find a way to stay creative and focused even though a lot of the gut feeling is sapped away by boy bands and billboards."

I glanced at Mark. My own work in the music industry was like my work everywhere else. I was a silent assistant to the fame of others. Exactly how I liked it. "People underestimate Mr. Homey. Perhaps they do not really understand him."

"That was what I was trying to say. Jack was the poet, and Randolph the musician; that is the truth as I see it." I took out a slip of paper and wrote on it a single sentence, then slid it across the table to Mark.

He looked at the paper, then up at me. "Are you sure you want me to give this to Randolph?"

"Do you think it is dangerous to do so?" I asked.

"From Randolph? I doubt he will read it or care. He is a musician, all the rest left when Jack disappeared." He left the thought in the air that danger might come from other directions. "Jack and the Portals was a long time ago. Randolph survived that time with his sanity, his reputation, his creativity, and his soul intact. And people still remember the Portals."

"But aren't you curious that there is another story to tell?" I asked.

We paid for the tea, and as we were leaving, Mark said, "Have you ever thought that some stories might be best left untold?"

I looked at him. "I guess there are songs best left unsung as well?"

He put his hand on his unshaven chin. "Don't wait by the phone." He left toward the library parking lot.

PONDERING RAVENS

Rackhar Zil, the Yellow King of Virdea has died, my ravens, and the Fell Wizard of the Great Obsidian Tower stirs forth seeking his domination of a human woman from the lands of Earth. Great forces move, and traps sit to becalm the heroes. Rndrl, I of the ravens Virdea, who declare conspiracy, do see that no end has come, only a pause in a story with many threats and threads lying exposed.

But is this the crack in time that was explained in prophecy? It is coming. I feel it, but the raven with the disrupted gears must reveal more to us. Good luck reader. Until the curtain rises again.

BOOK CLUB QUESTIONS

1. Why does Ivy press forward when the mission goes off the rails?

2. Why does an ascetic such as Rains-a-Lot find pride in hats?

3. Why does Dr. Kelle Brainerd dress in juvenile clothes when she has three doctorate degrees?

4. How does Violet interject herself into the group?

5. Which of the four main characters most represents the archetype of a hero to you?

6. Is the author real, or are the characters in the story real?

7. How does the ancient revolver used by Rains-a-Lot and the modern pistol by Ivy represent their dueling ideals of consciousness?

8. Does the demise of the Yellow King have any meaning to the story? If so, what?

9. What role does the souls corporation Dustin-Rhodes play in the story?

10. Is there any hidden meaning in the goals of the ravens?

AUTHOR BIO

Nelson McKeeby is a native of Iowa, born near Spirit Lake to a Navy Officer and a teacher. Placed in classes for slow learners at a young age, he was never able to make education work and left school by age sixteen. He immediately landed a job as one of the country's youngest live-air television directors and professional television writers, a career he has maintained since then. Nelson is neurodiverse with both autism and severe epilepsy. A long-time hitchhiker who often uses his experiences in his writing, he has also served with the Department of Justice and as a deputy sheriff.

Nelson is known for non-fiction writing about insider politics, law enforcement, the entertainment industry, and the Quaker faith. He splits his time between La Habra, California and Iowa, living with a Brazilian doctor of biology and nurse, and four cats in a multilingual household.

More books from 4 Horsemen Publications

Fantasy

D. Lambert
To Walk into the Sands
Rydan
Celebrant
Northlander
Esparan
King
Traitor
His Last Name

Danielle Orsino
Locked Out of Heaven
Thine Eyes of Mercy
From the Ashes
Kingdom Come
Fire, Ice, Acid, & Heart
A Fae is Done

J.M. Paquette
Klauden's Ring
Solyn's Body
The Inbetween
Hannah's Heart

Lou Kemp
The Violins Played Before Junstan
Music Shall Untune the Sky

R.J. Young
Challenges of Tawa

Sydney Wilder
Daughter of Serpents

Valerie Willis
Cedric: The Demonic Knight
Romasanta: Father of Werewolves
The Oracle: Keeper of the Gaea's Gate
Artemis: Eye of Gaea
King Incubus: A New Reign

Kyle Sorrell
Munderworld
Potarium

SciFi

Brandon Hill & Terence Pegasus
Between the Devil and the Dark
Wrath & Redemption

C.K. Westbrook
The Shooting
The Collision

NICK SAVAGE
Us Of Legendary Gods
So We Stay Hidden
The West Haven Undead

PC NOTTINGHAM
Mummified Moon

T.S. SIMONS
Project Hemisphere
The Space Between
Infinity
Circle of Protections
Sessrúmnir
The 45th Parallel

TY CARLSON
The Bench
The Favorite
The Shadowless

Milton Keynes UK
Ingram Content Group UK Ltd.
UKHW011824011223
433620UK00004B/258